Looking To Move On

Richard Frost

DEDICATION

For all who are looking to move on, may
you rise up on the wings of eagles.

Contents

Chapter 1 – Crossing the Road...1

Chapter 2 – Longer than the Boat Race...........................13

Chapter 3 – Forgiveness or What? 29

Chapter 4 – Pizza for one 45

Chapter 5 – We can all start again 63

Chapter 6 – Suspended 81

Chapter 7 – Tilly asks a question.......................................95

Chapter 8 – A reasonable risk...111

Chapter 9 – The power of love 131

Acknowledgements.. *145*

About the Author *147*

Credits *149*

CHAPTER 1

Crossing the Road

Wrapped in each other's arms, a head lies resting. The chest's gentle rise and fall accompanied by a rhythmic heartbeat. Hands are stroking hands.

Nearly dark. Two empty glasses on the table. The telly on mute.

Comfort. Security. Warmth.

The sound of a key in the lock breaks the silence.

'Daddy!'

Climbing down. Rushing out. Lifted up. Small arms wrap around a father's neck.

'Have a good time, sweetheart?' he asked.

The head that once rested nodded. 'We had ice cream!' she whispered. A secret pleasure.

'You had ice cream! Did you save me some?' he replied. 'Has she been okay, Mum?'

'We've had a great time.'

A look asked the silent question, 'Anyone?'

Her eyes replied, 'No, not yet'.

■   ■   ■

Matt West lifted his hands from the keyboard to reach for the mug of cold coffee sat on his desk. He liked the way the opening to his second novel could be misinterpreted. It reminded him of a song in the nineties by Cornershop about everybody needing a bosom for a pillow. He smiled at the thought of strait-laced members of his dad's church being appalled by the hint of a lovers' embrace – and what may have happened before or after.

A child with her grandma. Some will get it; others won't.

He wondered how the looks might lead the story. Whose eyes said what? Who are they waiting for? Ideas trickled, rather than flowed. The doctor calling about Grandad? The police saying they'd found… the dog, a child, a body? The bailiffs? It needed more work, but it was a start.

'What do you think, love?' Matt asked the photo next to the computer. The woman in the photo looked back.

Start. Power. Shut Down.

It was always a struggle to leave for work. The Housing Association had promised to install a power assisted door because manoeuvring his wheelchair was difficult. Matt was glad to live on the ground floor apart from when the chap opposite left his bike in the hallway.

Shoes secured (Velcro's easier than laces). Coat on. Bag on the back. Beanie. iPhone. He loved his music. All the decades. Aretha. Bacharach. Beyoncé. Billy Joel. Coldplay. Marley. All on his playlist. All in his story.

The November sunshine was bright and clear and the cold wind chafed his hands as they gripped and pushed. He'd forgotten his gloves again. A five-minute push for a five-minute bus ride. His strong upper body compensating for the weaker lower half.

Half an hour from the coast, Eastwood Minster is a large, busy, multicultural town, its population swollen by tourists in the summer and university students the rest of the year. Shops cater for West Indian and Asian tastes and the increase in Eastern European flavours. A green belt ensures weight gain from new builds is kept to a minimum. Parks and riverside walks aid the town's health and wellbeing. The 10th Century Minster Church stands proud in the centre alongside the river wending its way to the sea.

Locals called the 2B 'The Shakespeare Bus' because sometimes it didn't turn up. The drivers were usually helpful: stopping at the raised kerbs and lowering the ramp. Pushchair wars were a regular occurrence. Audible sighs accompanied the folding of ones used for shopping. Matt had got used to it by now but the eyes spoke. 'What are they saying when they look at me?' he wondered. People often stared at someone in a wheelchair. Sometimes out of pity. Sometimes out of disdain.

He'd worked the evening shift for four months now. Three days a week, three hours a day. It was better than nothing and supplemented Universal Credit. A great improvement on the 18 months or so he'd spent on the sick and he knew he'd get a better job one day. It was pretty much the same every time. Customers came and went. Some less than ten in a basket, others a trolley full. Matt had always been a smiler. He'd be the one to cheer up someone else's dreary day. He'd be the one to get children to say 'beep' as he scanned. Do to others as you would have them do unto you. Until someone complained he was being too friendly and he got told off by the manager.

A First at Oxford. A rowing Blue. Five years at a leading advertising agency. 'Marketing maketh the man', he used to joke. Married at 24. Dad at 26. Published at 27. Now 29. A till operator in a pound shop. Not quite the career move he had planned or hoped for.

Besides rowing, Matt had occupied his university days with History and English and couldn't quite get over how he got in. His calm laid back exterior portrayed an equally stable and placid interior. No one had ever seen him 'lose it': whatever, whenever or wherever 'it' might have been. With a body honed in the gym and on the Thames, Matt's six foot two frame, combined with his natural humour, scored high on the student likeability index. This well-developed protective layer hid a lack of confidence: especially where women were concerned. He had tried and failed, lusted and lost.

It was different with Jo McKenzie. A finals year romance. They'd met through the Christian Union: described by many as a dating agency for virgins, as indeed some were. Jo was a BA Fine Arts at The Ruskin School. Petite, quietly spoken, her shoulder length, auburn hair provided the perfect frame for her bespectacled face. Lots of other guys liked her and for a long time Matt thought he would probably lose out (again). She hated rowing though: nothing more boring to watch, she once said. A joint interest in art brought them closer. He preferred Hockney and Warhol. She liked Monet and Delacroix.

After leaving the city of dreaming spires, they moved on together but not in together. Shared faith meant shared restraint – although there were times when they wanted to, really wanted to. Jo got work at a National Lottery funded community arts project while Matt started with Wilson MacDonald. Designing ads for bus shelters wasn't top notch, but it was a start. Renting studio apartments only ten minutes' walk apart, Eastwood Minster provided a convenient commuting base for them both.

Matt's mum, Janice, a part-time social worker in Adult Services and his Pentecostal Pastor dad, Des, lived nearby. Matt was their only surviving child and Jo soon became the daughter they'd always wanted but never had.

Likewise, Rob and Gill McKenzie regularly welcomed Matt to their family home: a five-bedroomed detached in the heart of the Cotswolds. Both in their late fifties, Rob had taken a severance package from an investment bank in the City to live the dream of a long and happy retirement. Devoted to their two daughters, only the best was good enough and they always gave the best.

Three years after leaving university, Jo and Matt's wedding was the talk of the Cotswolds' glossy magazines when Des' gospel choir rolled into the small village church. The local vicar lamented it wasn't always like that on Sundays. The parishioners were less enthusiastic: 'Just not Church of England' they muttered. At least the organist had a sense of humour: playing a few bars of Village People's 'Go West' in honour of Jo's married name. Some got it; others didn't.

Once married, they moved in to a cramped, second floor, two-bed rented apartment not far from Matt's parents. It was cheap but it was home because they made it so. Tilly arrived a couple of years later and, girl, did they know it. All the things a baby brings and two floors up. Life was never the same again and they loved her all the more because of it.

Matt had begun his debut novel about a teenage activist caught up in the 1950s American Black civil rights movement before uni. His paternal grandparents had often told him about what happened in the States before they emigrated to the UK. Playing Sam Cooke's 'A Change Gonna Come' on their Dansette record player, their stories of racial segregation sparked a passion in Matt's heart whenever he visited them in the St Paul's area of Bristol.

He'd always admired the fact they'd carried on living there after the riot in April 1980. The trouble had started just down the road at the Black and White Café – the irony of the name was not lost on them. His grandparents told him how they were sat in their home in Albert Park. They could hear sirens outside and, in the days when listening to the police on FM radio was possible, they found out just how close it all was. Very close. Just at the end of the road. In the morning, the damage was clear. The bank was a burnt-out shell, as were other buildings – but none of the pubs. Cars lay wrecked and windows smashed. They told Matt how the young man next door at number 19 moved out soon afterwards because of it all. Many were injured and arrested although no one was ever convicted. It wrecked the area for a while and his grandparents played their part in supporting those who rebuilt it. The more he worked on his novel, the more he realised that racial tensions had always been prominent over here as well as in the States. He always knew Black lives mattered.

Study, rowing and meeting Jo had all intervened with writing the book, though, so when Tilly was in bed and Jo was out teaching evening classes, Matt picked up the story's threads and weaved them together.

■ ■ ■

The setting sun signed its autograph in red and orange pastels that warm June evening. The book launch had gone well. The publishers had marketed the marketing man. Early sales were promising but not yet second book stage. It was a half-hour walk from Waterstones to pick up Tilly from Matt's parents. She always enjoyed being with her grandma and grandad. Jo held Matt's arm as they walked. She on the inside, him by the kerb – ever the chivalrous.

'It was good so many people came, Matt. You did really well saying what you did and explaining about the background to the book. I wonder how many people have no idea what was going on in those times?' Jo wondered. 'Did you see the man in the bright red coat?'

'Yeah, I know. Quite something, wasn't it? White beard too,' replied Matt. 'Shame it isn't Christmas. You know what, though, he asked me to sign three copies – one for his partner, called Greg I think and two for his kids.'

Jo raised her eyebrows very slightly. 'I wonder what the kids think?'

'What, you mean because…'

'Yeah. It must have taken some getting used to. I guess they're very much loved all the same.'

'And I very much love you,' replied Matt.

Jo turned and kissed him. They looked at each other. It was 'The Look of Love', as Burt Bacharach and Hal David called it (or ABC, Matt joked to himself).

'How are you feeling about your job?' he asked, as they walked on arm in arm.

'It's difficult to know,' she replied. 'I enjoy it but constantly going from funding crisis to funding crisis is unsettling and takes the edge off things a bit. The managers are always stressed and going on about cost-effectiveness and where they can cut back. It's almost as if they're not interested in what we're actually doing anymore. It's such a shame, really.'

They crossed the road at the junction with Church Street. It was ten past nine. A bus pulled up at the lights.

'I'm looking to move on,' Jo said as they reached the other side.

The car was travelling over thirty in a twenty zone when it mounted the pavement.

Jo never felt a thing.

CHAPTER 2

Longer than the Boat Race

Matt felt no pain as he came around, but years of rowing told him his legs weren't right. As his eyes adjusted to the bright, late morning sunshine, the impact was darkened by the clinical surroundings of the hospital room.

He smiled at the sight of Gill McKenzie and Des West sitting at the bedside. Gill had brought Matt's iPhone and the photo of Jo. Des came with a small wooden cross. Comfort for body, mind and soul.

They looked. Looks that loved and lingered. Looks that had lost.

'Where's Jo?' Matt whispered.

Words weren't needed because their eyes spoke and Matt knew he'd never forget what they said. It was 'the day the music died', as Don McLean wrote.

'She never felt a thing, Matt,' Jo's mum said, her tears falling as their fingers intertwined. There was silence. An uncomfortably numb silence.

'Tilly?'

'She's fine.' Des replied reassuringly. 'She's with your mother. We've been taking it in turn to have her and to be here.'

'The doctors said the driver had a medical episode and lost control,' Gill explained because she thought Matt needed to know. 'No drink. No drugs. It was an accident. A terrible accident.'

Matt gave a silent nod. His mind both empty and full at the same time. 'Who was he?'

'He was called Greg. In his sixties.'

They sat. They stayed. The silence stayed also.

■　■　■

The first few mornings were always the same. Gradually waking from sleep, Matt would think about what he and Jo would do that day. And then he remembered as grief's disconnection between hope and stark reality crashed in.

The book. The pavement. Her kiss. The car. Over and over again. Without hesitation. Without deviation. And plenty of repetition. The memories lasted more than just a minute and none of it was funny. 'Why didn't I turn to protect her?' he'd ask himself with equal levels of reiteration. 'Why did I look round at the car instead of pushing her out of the way? It was my fault. What if I'd…'.

■ ■ ■

Sat by his bed a week later, the consultant tried hard to hide her feelings of awkwardness. Glasses perched on top of her short, dark brown hair, Doctor Jane Deshpande had treated many people with spinal cord injuries but this was hard. 'How do I tell him this when he's just lost his wife and there's a one year-old bairn?' she'd asked a colleague beforehand.

Matt appreciated the 'don't know what say' look although the band of gold on her left hand struck a painful spot. He smiled. 'Just tell me how it is.'

'Well, Matt. Can I call you Matt?' asked Dr Deshpande. 'I'm not going to tell you you'll never walk again. It's probably because you're fit and those years of rowing have given your legs strength to work with. The fact the ambulance was there within a few minutes, and they were able to put you in a neck collar and on a spine board helped. They got you here quickly too. In that respect,' she paused as she glanced at Jo's photo on the bedside cabinet. 'In that respect, you were lucky.'

Matt momentarily raised his eyebrows, unsure whether or not to believe her.

'Because the car hit you in the lower back, the damage to the spinal cord has caused a degree of paraplegia – paralysis below your waist.'

'Wait a minute.' Matt interjected, seemingly ignoring the news of his life-changing injury. 'You said it hit me in the back. I was looking at the car.'

'Well, no, Matt. Witnesses said you turned back to protect your wife.'

There was a long silence while Matt absorbed this sudden alteration to his repetitive, intrusive memory. He had to know. 'So, I was standing… standing, facing her… Was I holding her?'

'It seems so, Matt.'

Guilt gripped his stomach. A punch in the solar plexus. He struggled to find words. His breathing became more rapid.

His upper limbs and chest tightened. 'She died because I was holding her?' he said laboriously and painfully. The edge in his voice was tangible.

Jane Deshpande didn't hesitate to respond clearly and calmly: 'There'll be an inquest, and from what witnesses said and the paramedics reported, if anything, she broke your fall. She saved you, Matt.'

They said nothing while Matt endeavoured to absorb the tsunami of overwhelming emotions.

'Do you want me to come back later?' the consultant asked after a couple of minutes of recuperative quietness.

Shaking his head, Matt replied: 'Tell me about the walking.'

Doctor Deshpande knew not to overwhelm him as she explained the likely changes he'd experience over the coming days and weeks. How he'll transfer to a specialist spinal injuries unit in the hospital where physiotherapists will help with movement and how to sit upright without overbalancing. Matt laughed about the catheter and the new way of doing all that business.

'We can also provide counselling to help with the inevitable anger and loss,' she said in a very matter of fact way. 'My best guess at the moment – and it is very early days, Matt – is you'll be in hospital for anywhere between four and twelve months.'

'Longer than the Boat Race then,' Matt joked, knowing this particular journey would be a lot tougher than a row down the Thames. Months of training and hard work were facing him once more.

'With time, treatment and effort on your part,' the consultant concluded. 'We'll have you home, working and playing with your daughter again.'

The mention of Tilly brought waves of unstable emotions to the surface. They broke heavily on the shoreline of his mind. A baby with no mum and a crippled dad. It was the first time he'd cried. Really cried. A man's tears. Coming up from a depth that hurt. And Jo wasn't there to hold him.

■ ■ ■

Greg Dymond had never had a seizure before. The doctors said it was possible epilepsy. It sometimes starts in people of his age, they said. He remembered seeing the number

31 at the lights. The next thing he knew, two paramedics were inside his car, blue flashes disorientating his gradual regaining of consciousness. 'You're going to be okay,' a voice said. 'You've been in an accident and we're going to help you.' At least he thinks that was what she said.

If it hadn't been for the bus driver's emergency call and a passing doctor on the way to night shift, it would have been a lot worse, if such a thing was possible. The seizure had probably caused his right hand to come off the wheel and his leg to spasm and push down the accelerator.

It was a day or two before Ian told him about Jo and Matt West. Ian knew what it was like to tell someone else about a death as he'd done so to his sister when their elderly dad died after a long illness. But nothing like this. Ever.

They sat on the sofa. Ian held Greg's hand. He couldn't look him in the eyes. 'I need to tell you something about the accident, Greg.'

■　■　■

Both 62, it all started eight years previously when Ian was still married. They'd progressed from banter, to bar, to bed where each found something they'd never known before. They worked for the Council: Ian on the bins, Greg on the roads. Their daily routes often crossing each other in the spidery network of streets. Being verbally abused by pedestrians and car drivers formed a common bond.

Married to Beth for 32 years, Ian Mason had never been quite sure who he was. They were happy together, had two lovely kids, but deep down there was unacknowledged knowledge of something missing. Beth had been more than understanding, their children less so to begin with. Deep down, she had always sensed something but marriage had followed pregnancy and they'd stayed together.

Greg was the more camp. Deliberately so. Banter got him laughs and attention. He'd always known he was gay and was glad to be so, as Tom Robinson said. He'd been through his 80s' black moustache period and now sported a dyed blonde, number two cut and earring. His hi-vis workwear covered a growing beer gut although giving up smoking for Ian had been a major achievement. Loads of previous partners had left plenty of rubbish in his dustbin, all the same.

A street sweeper for 30 years, like many solitary workers the job gave him time to think. Having left school at 16 with a couple of O-levels, Greg had spent the last few years improving his intellectual inferiority complex. At home, he would often be found reading – always factual, never fiction. Listening to podcasts on his round was his latest distraction. He'd found a series about American history so Matt's novel would provide a new approach to a topic he'd previously known nothing about. He'd appreciated Ian getting it signed but after what had happened couldn't face reading it.

The accident put paid to work. Because he was a lone worker, the Council said he couldn't do his round in case he had another seizure. They'd also have to wait for the medication to take effect and get advice from doctors and occupational health. Six months on full pay and six on half was the only lining in Greg's stormy cloud.

Since the accident, he'd not been out much with Ian and not at all by himself. He was afraid something would happen and no one would be there to help. He'd sit on the sofa so he could fall without hurting himself. Like two badly behaved dogs, depression and anxiety had both moved in. One sat on him while the other bit. Panic attacks scared him more than the desolation of the black moods. He wasn't going to admit about them to anyone – after all who wants that on their sick note? Epilepsy is bad enough.

The absence of daytime company and all the usual routine, fresh air and people contact took its toll on Greg. They were long days. Ian left at five to start the six o'clock shift and didn't get back until just before tea. Greg longed to be insulted by someone to give him some sense of normality. So, he insulted himself to make up for it. Rants to an empty house. 'Is this punishment, God, for being queer?' 'Come on, you're the effing council, you've got loads of jobs I could do.' 'Why were those two walking there in the first place?'

It was also tough on Ian. He didn't know which Greg he'd be coming home to (although it helped having been a husband and a dad). Between the silences and Greg's grunts when hearing about Ian's day, they'd have the same conversation over and over again. They'd argue more than ever, often over small things: like the time when Ian hung the washing on the sofa because there was nowhere else. No matter how many times he was told it wasn't his fault, Greg couldn't let go of the facts. He'd killed one person, disabled another and messed up himself. And now he was hurting the only man who'd ever really loved him. Matt West wasn't the only one who had been paralysed.

■ ■ ■

As the months passed, Matt made good progress at The Spinal Injuries Centre. The daytime routine was demanding and the staff balanced reality with encouragement. Spending the day in a wheelchair was better than lying in the rather uncomfortable hospital bed. Gym and hydrotherapy sessions were a great morale booster for the rower in him. He enjoyed the exercises and the fact he could tell he was making progress: doing a little bit more each days (well, most of them). It was good to know his upper body was still strong even though the lower half wasn't. Physio was hard at times but it was paying off: sit to stand was taking shape in a way he'd never thought possible a few weeks before. The staff often told him it was down to the rowing: not just physically but mentally too. He'd passed Craven Cottage but it was still a long way to Chiswick Bridge. It was tough going when he felt the tide was against him.

Indeed, there were days when the calm, laid back Matt felt anger like never before. He felt he was changing in to a different person and he didn't like it. He'd felt angry with Wilson Macdonald who gave four weeks sick pay and then sacked him on grounds of no longer being capable of doing his job. 'Rubbish,' he thought: 'I sit at a desk all day – my brain and arms still work, you know,' he'd rant to himself. However, he knew he was better off out of the job if that was how they fulfilled their duty of care.

He'd get frustrated at the lack of control he had over his body, though. The weakness. The exhaustion. The mess. The loss of motivation. The pain (the only bit which sometimes had a quick fix). He 'lost it' a few times when 'it' all became too much. Quick to apologise to the staff (who had seen it all before, of course), nevertheless, such incidents felt like his boat was sinking.

There were plenty of 'Why me?' questions that didn't get answers. Knowing Jo was in the best place didn't lessen his rage against God for taking her there. His grief for Jo was an overwhelming, ever-present dark shadow. The loss and the manner of it had ripped a hole in his heart which would never be filled. Yet he didn't want to spend the rest of his life feeling bitter: he'd met many others whose anger had eaten away their very soul. Counselling helped him understand such feelings and that they needed as much work as the exercises, just like the consultant had said. He was in it for the long haul.

One of his fellow rowers at university, Will Taylor, texted or talked through FaceTime once a week during the whole of the period Matt was in hospital. Will had been devastated to hear what had happened. Because Matt couldn't go to the funeral, it was Will who read out what he'd written about Jo. Will had been Best Man at their wedding and one of very few to keep in touch in those post-Oxford years.

Jo's parents visited the hospital once a fortnight. It was a long, awkward journey. Two hours if they were lucky, four if not. The toll of losing their eldest daughter was tangible and Matt saw how they'd aged. Tears flowed every time and he wished they wouldn't keep apologising for it. Jo's sister, Penny came occasionally. Younger, she bore a striking and at times disconcerting resemblance to her sibling. Petite, just like Jo, she had the same auburn hair and the same bespectacled face. Parenting is costly and Rob and Gill had paid the highest price: with interest charged every day for the rest of their lives.

Once a month, they arranged to be there at the same time as Matt's parents and it was good they could all see Tilly together. Living down the road from Minster Hospital, Des and Janice came at least twice a week and always brought Tilly along too. They found it tiring having her living with them all the time, and it was helpful that members of Des' congregation regularly called on them and brought clothes and toys for their granddaughter. Others would baby sit or take Tilly out to the park or down by the river to give them a break. It was hard for Matt to miss so much of Tilly growing up. The visits were a highlight, though, and provided added motivation to put in the work towards his recovery.

As the weeks went by, Tilly progressed from crawling to standing, and taking her first tentative steps, wondering if she'd fall over, just like her Dad. And she did, just like her Dad. She enchanted the staff with her big smile and hairband with a bow sitting over her black locks. She would sit on Matt's lap, and there was no better feeling. 'Row, row, row the boat, gently down the Thames,' he'd sing.

'Have they talked about when you'll leave here, Matt?' Janice asked one day.

'Yeah, they've said maybe in April, once I've found somewhere to live.' Matt had known straight away he'd never be able to return to the flat he'd shared with Jo. All their belongings had been moved into a friend's garage for safekeeping and he didn't look forward to the day when he'd see all she had left behind.

'You know there's a crowdfunding page?' blurted out Des, waking from forty winks in one of the high-backed hospital armchairs.

Janice gave him a look that was very clear in its meaning. 'Someone set it up,' Janice explained with a sigh. 'We don't know who but it's there. And there's a lot of money too. We weren't going to tell you until we knew what was happening.'

'That's right, all very hush, hush,' Matt's father responded trying to redeem himself.

Matt smiled, a cheeky glint in his eyes. '"Baby's father widowed and paralysed in car crash – unemployed and homeless". Makes for a good story, doesn't it?'

'Son of a well-known, local church minister,' Des added with typical, self-mocking humour. 'Don't forget that bit!' The laughter swept away the remaining awkwardness.

'And we don't know who it is?' Matt asked.

'No, not yet,' Janice replied. 'They seem to have some inside knowledge about how you're getting on and it's not coming from us. The website just says they'll make the money available when you leave hospital. There are so many lovely comments on it, Matt. People offering help for when you and Tilly get home. Some saying they'd be happy to bring meals or help move your furniture and belongings. And, you know, what's particularly special is that no one has said anything bad about the driver.'

'That is good, Mum,' replied Matt, 'especially given what social media can be like.'

The kindness of strangers both intrigued and touched him.

CHAPTER 3

Forgiveness or What?

Returning home on the 2B that cold November afternoon, Matt was looking forward to seeing Sophie Howlett, his Community Liaison Nurse. She'd visited him twice in hospital and had come to his home every other Friday since he was discharged. Tilly and his mum would be there too this time.

Sat on the bus, Matt thought about how much he'd enjoyed living in the two-bedroomed flat since he left hospital in April. With his furniture and belongings moved in, it was good to be surrounded by familiar possessions. Although ultimately cathartic, going through Jo's belongings was as poignant and as difficult as he'd feared. Jo had always dressed beautifully, and quirkily at times, with bright colours, sometimes matching, other times in deliberate contrast. Matt felt she'd be pleased a lot went to the clothes bank at the community centre run at his dad's church. It felt like he was throwing her away, all the same. He kept some of her earrings and bracelets for when Tilly was older and held on to a rainbow-coloured cashmere scarf for added comfort at day and at night.

An online deposit of £26,241 arrived via his publisher just after he moved in. Earlier in the week, Matt received a text from Sophie to ask if the people who'd raised it could come with her to meet him. It was then that he realised for the first time that she'd been the one with insider knowledge: she knew who the crowdfunders were. He had told Sophie a few months ago that he wished he could meet the people who had raised the money and was pleased that he could now do so.

He thought a lot about Sophie. He'd talked to her about more things than anyone else since losing Jo. She had been key in securing the purpose-built flat with its height-adjustable sink, grab handles and wide doorways. She'd got the Jobcentre people to pay for alterations to the till he used at work. Sophie also sourced a lighter wheelchair, bought with the crowdfunding money, and helped him with techniques from using the wet room to hanging up his clothes. On some visits, they'd go into town and practise shop entrances, kerbs and crossing the road. 'Just like I'll be doing with Tilly, I expect,' Matt would observe dryly. It was hard going along Church Street for the first time. Remains of flowers still held on tightly to a lamp post near the lights and Matt wondered who had put them there.

Sophie and Matt had talked about the inquest and how it was deemed to be accidental death. Jo had died instantaneously from a fractured skull as she hit the ground, so it was comforting to know she'd not suffered. Matt had found all the 'firsts' difficult. The first Christmas. The first time it was his birthday without her. The first time it was Jo's without her. Sophie knew how tough those times were and took a lunch break to visit Matt on the first anniversary of Jo's death to check he was as okay as he could be. He wasn't but it was good to have her there for a while.

On another occasion they met after work and celebrated his new publishing contract with a hot chocolate at Costa. They also chatted and laughed about how she went to university in Cambridge (Anglia Ruskin, that is). A year or two younger, Sophie was slim, pretty and had long blonde hair. Matt noticed her left hand and had to stop himself humming 'Single Ladies' by Beyoncé. He even wondered if he could put a ring on it but that felt like he was betraying Jo. 'It's not even 18 months: it's too soon to like someone else,' he'd tell himself. Sophie never mentioned anyone but, there again, he's a patient not a friend so why should she. All the same, it was good to know he was still able to have such thoughts. Deep down he didn't know whether he would ever love or be loved again.

Arriving home, Matt looked through the window. Tilly's head rested on her grandma's breast. Tilly first saw her dad's new home on her second birthday a couple of weeks after he'd moved in. They all ate ice cream to celebrate. Tilly was two and a half now and had begun to stay overnight when Matt wasn't working or didn't have hospital appointments. She had her own bedroom and eventually would live with him instead of at his parents. Tilly loved her grandparents, although she was looking forward to being with her dad all the time. Matt knew he'd have to tell her about Jo some time and that she would start asking more questions too. Other kids at nursery were picked up by their grandparents so it wasn't that unusual for her at the moment.

For now, she was safe in her grandma's arms. They stroked each other's hands. It was nearly dark. Two empty glasses stood on the table. The telly was on mute. The sound of a key in the lock heralded excitement.

'Daddy!' Tilly shouted, as she rushed over to him. Climbing on to his lap, she wrapped her small arms around his neck.

'Have a good time, sweetheart?'

The head that once rested nodded. 'We had ice cream!'

'You had ice cream!' Matt exclaimed. 'Has she been okay, Mum?'

'We've had a great time,' replied Janice.

Matt's eyes asked, 'Anyone?'

Janice replied, 'No, not yet'.

'Oh good, I thought I was going to be late. The bus was so crowded.' Matt took off his coat and put his bag down before going into the kitchen to make cups of tea. Tilly followed, showing him the plastic animals Grandma bought when they went to the shops. They'd got some cake too. It was warm in the flat, a welcome contrast to the cold wind which had seeped into Matt's bones. His gloves lay on the dining table.

The intercom sounded and Tilly picked it up. She'd learnt how to push the button to open the outside front door.

The one to the flat was too heavy, so she swung on the handle while Sophie pushed from the other side. Tilly liked Sophie. 'Come and see my animals,' she chattered excitedly. 'Can we play farms?'

As had become their routine, Sophie stood in the open door and then knelt and looked Tilly in the eyes: 'Dad first. Then you. Yes?'

'Yes!' yelled Tilly. She'd not quite got the hang of a high five and they were still working on it.

Sophie smiled at Matt as he came out of the kitchen towards her. He felt a gentle lift in his heart. He knew she'd like the fact he had a tray of drinks balanced on his lap, albeit somewhat precariously.

'Hi Matt,' said Sophie. She moved her right arm to indicate the crowdfunders lingering behind her in the shadows of the now darkened hallway.

'I think you've met Ian. This is Greg.'

■ ■ ■

It had taken an enormous effort for Greg Dymond to feel able to meet Matt. He had another seizure about six weeks after the accident and a third one four months later. Tweaks in the medication had kept him stable since then although being off sick for so long was frustrating. Now approaching the end of Statutory Sick Pay, while Ian said they'd be alright, Greg worried about the money. He'd had regular meetings at work. His manager was helpful and understanding but her hands were tied waiting for occupational health reports which were many and far between. Human Resources kept talking about risk and capability: however, in his favour Greg was known to be a reliable worker who had never had a day off sick before all this happened. He was hoping he might get ill health retirement although knew they didn't give that to people that much these days.

Ian had heard about something called Cognitive Behavioural Therapy and Greg had finally let Ian help him to contact the NHS talking therapies service to deal with the worsening depression and increasing anxiety. After only a few sessions, although he went on to have more, Greg began to gradually gain better control of his feelings. The anger subsided and while the cloud that mentally hung over him still brought occasional heavy showers, there were a lot more sunny intervals.

He'd been going out on his own too. Just to the end of the street at first then to Tesco Express and the bookies. He would wear Ian's red coat for added confidence. Sunny days, even when it was cold, meant going to the local park – it was quite a walk and caused him anxiety especially if a car came around a corner at high speed. The views over the river and surrounding parkland made it worthwhile and he would often just sit, listening to the birds in the trees and watching others on the river. It was a good place to read a book too. Tranquillity for a still troubled mind.

He remembered a Deacon Blue song about a worker for the council who 'picked litter off the gutter'. Greg knew he'd eventually have his ship called Dignity too. All the same, he struggled with whether or not Matt West would ever forgive him for what he'd done. Greg had never really known what it was to be forgiven by anyone. He'd hurt lots of people along the way and many he used to know now passed him by on the other side of the road, literally as well as metaphorically.

■ ■ ■

With Ian at the wheel, as they drove home from Matt's that evening, tears ran down Greg's face and moistened the beard he'd grown since stopping work. The silence in the car at odds with the noise of the rush hour. He'd not known what to expect – apart from probably being shouted at. Which would have been for good reason, he thought: after all he had killed this man's wife and left him in a wheelchair.

Greg had put on his best suit to try and give a better impression. He was so nervous about going and, although he wouldn't admit it, not even to Ian, had been terrified about how Matt would react. It had taken all his effort not to shout at Ian for pushing him into going.

'Well, I never expected that,' Greg said at last. 'I mean, how on earth can someone talk to me like that. To say those things. I mean, it's not normal, is it?'

'No, that's right, love, it's not,' replied Ian, pulling up the car outside their home.

'I do know it wasn't my fault,' said Greg. Ian looked at him: it was the first time his partner had ever said that. 'Well, at least it wasn't deliberate.' Ian smiled at the qualifying comment. 'I just can't believe he didn't even ask me to explain what in hell's name I was doing,' Greg continued. Ian held in the thought that whispered, 'Here we go again, he's pressing the repeat button.'

'He didn't even seem angry,' Greg continued. 'I was waiting for him to yell at me all the time we were there.

Especially when I saw the kid and his mum: I thought they're really going to pull at the heart strings. And then there was tea and cake – softening us up and all that. They're really going to make us suffer.'

'But they didn't, did they?' added Ian pragmatically.

'No, I know and I can't understand it. I mean, how he said it was lovely to meet me. No one ever says that to me – except you. And then straight in. No messing, was there? What was it he said? How he couldn't even begin to understand what it had been like for me. This should have been about him, not me – what he'd been through: not me.'

'Yeah, I know,' said Ian. 'And when he said he wanted you to know he didn't blame you. I could have cried.'

'You could have cried? I could have wept buckets, mate. I mean is that forgiveness or what?'

They held hands as they looked through the car's windows. The wipers intermittently clearing away the rain that trickled down the windscreen. 'What a doll of a girl, that Tilly. I could run off with her quite easily,' Greg laughed for the first time that week.

'His mum was lovely too, wasn't she?' said Ian. 'You remember when you said how scared you'd been about coming?'

'Yeah, what was it she said: "Perfect love casts out fear" was it? Shakespeare or someone?'

'Bible, I think, Greg.'

'Oh yeah, that would make sense, them being church people and all that. Forgive us our trespasses, eh?'

'Indeed.'

'I tell you what though. I mean I still feel bad about what happened, obviously, and I'll never forget it, but it's lifted off a great load knowing that, well, you know…'

'I know, Greg. I know.'

■ ■ ■

After everyone else had gone, Sophie and Tilly played farms on the rug in front of the gas fire. 'Pandas, giraffes and cows in the same barn, Tilly. Wow!'

'They've all got to sleep somewhere, Sophie,' said Tilly knowingly. 'Now, time for your sleep. This is your bed,' she said pointing at the sofa. 'I'll get you a doo... a doo... very... so you don't get cold. It's got Olaf on it.'

'Oh! From Frozen. That's my favourite film,' Sophie replied. 'Thank you, Tilly, but I think I should be going now. After all, it must be nearly time for your tea.'

'Would you like something to eat, Sophie?' asked Matt, sat on the sofa watching them. 'I do a pretty good salad in the microwave,' he joked.

'Daddy's silly,' his daughter said, as they all laughed.

'That's kind of you, thanks, Matt,' replied Sophie. 'I've got to go and see my dad, I'm afraid.'

'Another time, perhaps?' Matt said hesitantly. She looked at him. Bungled that one, he thought.

'Matt,' now Sophie was the one to hesitate. 'I've got a new job. It's on the same team so it means that I'll be handing over your ongoing care to a colleague. I'm afraid this is my last visit – but I wanted you to meet Greg before I finished. It took a long time to organise.'

Matt found it hard to hide his sadness. 'Oh, I'm sorry to hear that, but glad for you – is it a promotion?'

'It is actually. I'm going to be managing the team I'm currently in. So bit less hands on, which I'll miss. It'll be good, though, I think.'

They looked at each other, aware of the boundaries. They'd grown close – or at least Matt had towards Sophie: he didn't know if it was reciprocated. He hoped it might be. He didn't want to lose someone else.

Sophie had made him feel as if he was the only patient she had. He told her that once – she'd replied saying that was one of the greatest compliments a health worker could have. She only wished some of her other patients realised they weren't the only one.

There was an awkward pause. 'Might I see you sometime? As a friend?' Matt asked, feeling he had nothing to lose but fearing he may do so.

Sophie looked at him and smiled. 'I'd like that, Matt. I'd like that'.

'Great!' Matt found it hard to hide his surprise and wasn't sure if he believed her either. He remained doubtful about whether anyone still liked him given how he was now. 'Text me?'

'Yes. I will. Thank you.'

'And thank you. I wouldn't be where I am today if it wasn't for you, Sophie.'

'Well, I'm glad I've been of some help,' she said, picking up both her bag and her professionalism. 'I'm just doing my job but it's always good when people make progress – that's what makes it worthwhile. You've worked really hard to get yourself where you are – a lot of people don't do that. Anyway, I'll ask my colleague, Steve Dawson to get in touch and he'll come and see you before Christmas. He's a nice chap and very good at his job.'

'Thanks for bringing over Ian and Greg,' said Matt, trying to prolong her presence. 'That was very special. I didn't know quite what they'd be like – I thought they may be defensive and it might be awkward. I wanted him to know I wasn't angry with him and that he was, well, forgiven, in a way. Not that he'd done anything wrong, really. It was so kind of them – and all the people on the Council who contributed that money and the LGBT community too. It was so generous.'

'It was Ian who pushed it along,' explained Sophie, who didn't really want to go either, despite now wearing her coat. 'They told Greg's consultant what they'd done and she tracked me down. Initially, Ian and Greg didn't want you to know who was behind it, so I suggested they ask your publisher to act as middleman. Confidentiality was never broken, Matt, although I did pass on what you said a while ago about wishing you could meet them. It took Greg a long time to feel he could come, though.'

Tilly climbed on to Matt's lap. 'Well, thanks again, Sophie.'

Wrapping a rainbow-coloured scarf around her neck, Sophie smiled. 'Yep. See you soon.'

Matt watched the door closing behind her. He could feel a lump in his throat and a tear forming. Someone else had moved on from his life.

'I like Sophie,' said Tilly interrupting his melancholy. 'Do you like Sophie, Daddy?'

'Yes, Tilly, I do.' A touch of sadness dampened the inflection in his voice.

'Is she going to be my Mummy?' asked Tilly. A touch of innocence in hers.

Matt laughed as he reached for the photo which stood by the computer: 'This is your Mummy, Tilly.'

'Pretty lady.'

'Yes, she is,' replied Matt, bracing himself for the first of the conversations he'd be having for many years to come.

'I like her.' Tilly looked at the photo. Drawing her finger around Jo's face, down her nose and across her mouth. 'Nice hair.'

Matt waited. Waiting for the right time to explain. Tilly's head rested on his chest and stroked the hairs on his arm.

'Tea time!' she shouted.

CHAPTER 4

Pizza for one

The first couple of months had been a steep learning curve for Sophie. It was taking some of the team time to adjust to the change from her being a colleague to becoming their manager – although she tried to be both. It was strange having her own office and Sophie spent as little time in it as possible in order to still feel part of the team. There'd been a lot to think about and she was looking forward to a week's leave, even though it was the end of January (she'd not taken time off over Christmas due to staff shortages). From Steve Dawson's reports in the weekly case conferences, she knew Matt was doing well but she hadn't been in touch.

After calling home to get changed and pick up an overnight bag, Sophie drove the short distance to one of the new housing estates where Dave Rawlinson lived. She let herself in with the key he'd given her. Spotting another Ikea purchase in the hallway, she took off her coat and put it with her bag. Entering the lounge, Sophie watched Dave coming towards her from the kitchen. Her heartbeat quickened.

'Good evening, Nurse Howlett,' he said, closing the laptop on the dining table as he approached. 'Good evening, Detective Constable.' They kissed. The bag stayed downstairs.

She'd always been looking for love. Her mother left the family home when Sophie was Tilly's age, hadn't been seen since and Sophie had never known why. Throughout her childhood, her dad was loving and caring and worked long hours to keep them in house and home. She saw her grandparents a lot but once at school, Sophie and her older sister were latchkey children right through their teenage years. Sophie did well at school and college and her dad was immensely proud when she was accepted for nurse training. University was a succession of placements and parties, lectures and lovers. It was exciting at the time (and had been so since) bouncing from one man to another like a ball in a tennis match. The result was never love all.

Sophie remained close to her dad who now had early onset dementia and needed full-time care. The last few months had found her stranded at life's crossroads: struggling to find the signpost let alone read it. She was, as Kirsty MacColl sang, 'looking for another girl.'

She had not had much luck with men – nor they with her, she thought – until she met Dave Rawlinson. He was handsome, a few years older and greatly admired in the local community. He had a bit of a reputation as a ladies' man, but Sophie ignored those who told her to be careful: she was proud of her 'catch' and vowed to hold on to him, unlike others. This is 'the one', she thought (again).

That evening, Sophie was wrapped in his arms. Her head lay on his chest. It's gentle rise and fall accompanied by a rhythmic heartbeat. Hands stroking hands. Two empty glasses stood on the bedside table and the telly was on mute.

Dave used his smartphone to order a pizza online, dressed and went downstairs to the kitchen to pour some more wine. Looking at her mobile as she followed, Sophie saw she had two missed calls. She sat at the dining table and began opening the laptop. 'I'll just see what's on...'

'No!' shouted Dave. One arm outstretched in her direction, his other hand instinctively went to his belt. Poised to arrest.

'Oh! Pardon me, officer,' she said with a touch of sarcasm and a grip of fear.

Stand-off.

'Sorry,' said Dave. 'I shouldn't have said it like that.' ('How should you have said it, then, Dave?' thought Sophie.) 'Please don't touch it,' he added with a smile.

She remembered what Matt's mum had said: 'perfect love casts out fear'. This was not perfect love. And she was afraid.

The doorbell rang. 'That'll be our pizza.' Dave said with a feigned smile as he shut the hall door behind him.

It only needed a look.

'Pizza for one, is it?' said Sophie, as he returned. She could feel anger rising up inside her.

'What do you mean?' he replied innocently, his professional coolness restored.

Sophie pointed to the now fully open laptop: 'Explain.' A single word spoke a thousand of them.

'Oh, that. It's alright, Soph,' laying on the charm again. 'Nothing to worry about. I thought it might be a bit of fun.'

'Fun!' Sophie exploded with a rage she had never ever felt before. 'So, I'm your bit of fun, am I?' she shouted. 'I'm not good enough so you get your kicks from these pictures, do you? I'm your sex toy, am I? Someone to act out your fantasies with? Is that what happened to all the other women you've had? Do they all have keys? Do they all get wined, dined and bedded? Well, no more Detective Constable David Rawlinson.'

Standing up, the chair fell backwards with a crash as she strode towards to the hall door. With an upper cut that would have pleased any prize fighter, she hit the pizza box he was holding. The contents splattered the policeman's shirt and provided the perfect topping for the offending laptop.

'Bitch,' he yelled as he grabbed Sophie's arm. She knew he was stronger than her and his grip hurt. She felt his uncut nails digging into her skin. But he wasn't the only one who'd done control and restraint training. With a swift movement of her arm and a perfectly targeted heel, she released herself, ran to the hall, grabbed her coat and bag and slammed the front door behind her.

Breathing heavily. She was shaking. Her heart beating so strongly it felt as if it was going to leap out of her chest. She stopped for a moment in the pouring rain. Another missed call. Rosie. His brand new Alfa Romeo stood on the drive. Not a scratch on it. 'So, you're an Alfa Romeo are you?' she said to herself as she stood there. 'Well, I am not your Beta Juliet.' Sophie reached for the front door key. She gripped it tightly in her hand. So tight it left a mark. She knew what she was going to do. Right there. Right now.

Dave Rawlinson was eating pizza as the letterbox clattered.

When it came in at 8.53, the text was a surprise.

Hi Matt, sorry it's so late. Can I come round? Sophie

Matt had known only too well what 'see you soon' often meant in reality, so he was pleased to hear from her. Steve Dawson was as good as Sophie said he would be although he had only visited twice – once before Christmas and again a couple of weeks ago. On the second occasion, he told Matt he would be discharged next month: such is the paradox of improvement and progress – and increasing caseloads. He could still get in touch if he needed help, Steve had told him.

January had been a good month for Matt. Work had been okay and the awkward colleagues were being more civil too – he thinks senior management had 'had a word'. The bus passengers were much the same, though.

The intercom buzzed at quarter past nine. It was the first time Sophie had seen Matt standing. She'd forgotten how much taller he was. A good eleven inches. 'Sorry to land on you like this,' she said. 'All very unethical – I just needed someone to be with.'

'That's fine, Sophie. It's lovely to see you.' She was cold, wet and shaking. Her usual pristine hair was a mess and he could see she'd been crying: 'What's happened?'

'My dad's died.'

Leaning one of his crutches against the lounge wall, Matt held the freed arm open wide and Sophie stepped into the safe space he'd created for her. They held each other for a couple of minutes: longer than Matt had stood since the accident. His heart beating faster from the compassion he felt for her loss. His grief absorbing hers. Eventually, he asked to sit down. 'Sorry, yes of course,' said Sophie as she touched the wet patch on his shirt.

'It's seen worse,' replied Matt as he lowered himself into his wheelchair. Sophie smiled. She took off her coat and he noticed her arm. He could see the imprint of fingers and a long reddening scratch.

'Would you like a coffee?' he asked.

'Anything stronger?'

'J2O?'

Sophie smiled again. 'Coffee will be fine. Black please.'

Matt's flat was totally different to the posh new build she had recently left. Full of charity shop furniture and hand me downs. Three chairs at the dining table, two of them matching. The TV stood on an upside-down, vintage orange crate which used to belong to his grandparents. Bookshelves had found the computer desk a welcome source of support. A wooden coffee table stood in front of a large sofa, with its cushions of all sizes and colours. The newest thing was a turntable – sat atop his dad's large speakers with their ground-shaking subwoofer. Back in the eighties, they blasted reggae in the streets of St Paul's. Now, they were bookends for a vinyl collection. They still worked but hadn't played anything since the day the music died.

'It's good to see you, Matt. I'm sorry I've not been in touch – it's been hectic at work. I'd heard you were standing now. That's great.'

'Yeah, with these things,' he said, pointing to his crutches as he wheeled himself over to the kettle. 'Anyway, what about you?'

'How long have you got?'

'As long as you want,' he replied. 'Can you give me a hand with the mugs first – I've not passed the two cups and crutches exam yet.'

Sat on the three-seater sofa, Sophie adjusted the cushions placing one across her chest and holding it firmly with her arms. She drew up her knees and rested her chin on the cushion. Tears flowed again. Matt pulled himself towards her, 'Is it okay if…' he said looking at the space at the other end. He knew how valuable it was to sit at the same level as other people.

'Yes, of course, Matt. That's fine. It's been a nightmare evening. Not quite sure where to start really.' She reached out a hand towards the coffee table and took a sip from her drink. 'I've been seeing this guy for a few weeks and I thought everything was okay. He seemed lovely. Wined, dined, gave me flowers. I went to his house after work and something didn't feel quite right. He seemed a bit… but then he turned on the charm and all seemed okay again. Later on, he got really angry when I went to look at his laptop – I just wanted to see what was on at the cinema.' She took another sip. The mug provided welcome warmth.

'I've done some pretty weird things with men, Matt.' Sophie paused wondering if she might have offended the pastor's son. 'What I saw was horrible. Disgusting. He obviously had it in mind that we'd do it. I got really angry. I know I've got a bit of a temper at times but it's never that bad. I've never felt anything like it in my life. I tried to get out and he grabbed hold of my arm.' Sophie paused, consciously touching where it hurt.

'I think I must have kicked him, so I managed to escape. I was… I was really frightened. I didn't know what he'd do next. So, I just ran. I haven't run so fast for years. In my heels too,' she said with a slight laugh. 'I got back to my car. Dead scared. I even locked the doors from the inside. I knew I had missed calls. It was my sister, Rosie. She told me Dad had died an hour or so before.'

Sophie paused. A tissue dried her tears. Matt listened in silence. A gentle look to comfort her. His company providing safety and security.

'There I was,' she continued, 'there I was in bed with that monster as my dad died.' She paused again. 'Maybe he was right, maybe I am a bitch. I wish I had keyed his car. I am so naïve, Matt. Thinking a policeman would make me feel more secure. Good old Nurse Howlett can certainly pick the wrong men.'

Still holding the cushion, Sophie shuffled herself over and leant her head on Matt's shoulder. Tears flowing once more.

'Oh, Sophie,' said Matt after a while. 'Sounds like you're best away from him, though.' He felt Sophie's head gently nodding. 'Had your dad been unwell?'

Sophie sat upright. Put the cushion to one side and picked three long blond hairs off Matt's shirt. 'Yeah, he has… had early onset dementia and live-in carers. Mum left us when I was tiny and my sister's been great. Rosie lives just around the corner from him and has done virtually everything. In one sense, it wasn't a surprise.'

'Is that near here?'

'It's an hour's drive, so not too bad. I used to go over about once a week – usually after work on a Friday. Got that one wrong, today, didn't I?' chastising herself once more.

'Hey, you did what you did, Sophie,' said Matt reassuringly. 'Sometimes these things don't work out as we'd like.'

'You're telling me,' she replied, leaning her head on his shoulder again. 'I'm so glad you were in. Apart from work

I don't really know anyone else – no offline friends. I've always admired your kindness, Matt, and how you dealt with what happened to you. I knew… I knew I could come to you and it would be okay… you wouldn't… to be frank, you wouldn't be yet another man trying to get me into bed. Sorry to put it like that.'

Matt moved his other hand, gently placing it on her arm. 'I'm glad you felt that way. Have you eaten? How about some microwaved salad?'

Sophie laughed. 'Beans on toast?'

Replaying the evening's events in her mind and out loud, Sophie tried to eat. Matt cleared up while Sophie went to his room to phone her sister. Their dad had died peacefully at home with Rosie and a carer by his side. Rosie said it had been a privilege to be with him at that moment. She was waiting for the doctor to come to certify the death and for the funeral director to take their dad's body away.

'I'm going over to see her tomorrow afternoon,' Sophie told Matt after the call. 'We can have a chat then about the funeral and what else needs to be done.'

'That'll be good. She'll find that helpful too,' Matt observed as they sat on the sofa again. 'My and Jo's parents did everything cos I couldn't. It's good to have others around.' He paused. The memory of the unattended funeral lingering once again in his mind. 'Now, how about you? What are you going to do now?

Sophie shrugged her shoulders. 'I don't know, really. I don't particularly want to be on my own, to be honest.'

'Okay,' said Matt. 'Now don't take this the wrong way, Sophie, but I can offer you the sofa if you wanted to stay here.' Sophie thought for a moment. She didn't take it the wrong way.

'I'll get you one of Tilly's duvets. She's in a bed now. One with a side gate to stop her falling out. You can imagine what it's like when she does – me trying to help her in my state. I'll get you the one with Olaf on it if you like.'

Sophie smiled. Grateful for kindness and a safe place. She went to her car and brought in her bag.

'So-pheeeee!' Tilly emerged from her bedroom the next morning and jumped on the sofa. 'You've got my duvet. You are a naughty lady,' she said unperturbed by the unexpected presence.

'Oh, I'm sorry, Tilly. Your Daddy gave it to me,' explained the visitor.

'Well, he's a very naughty man,' replied Tilly as Matt came into the room.

'I see Tilly's woken you up, then,' he said.

'It's okay, Matt, I was already awake. Morning.'

'My Mummy's gone to heaven,' Tilly announced with no preamble.

Sophie smiled and looked her in the eyes. 'Well, you know what, Tilly. My Daddy's just gone to heaven too.'

Tilly's eyes opened wide. 'Oh! Do you think they'll see each other? What do you think they'll have for breakfast? I like Coco Pops. Are you staying for breakfast?'

'I'd like that very much, Tilly. Have you got any cornflakes?'

'Nope,' Tilly replied firmly. 'We've got… umm,' placing an index finger to her mouth. 'Rice Krispies. Toast. Boiled egg – with soldiers. Ice cream.'

'I think I'll have all of those, Tilly, I'm very hungry,' the guest replied.

'All of them!' expressed Tilly in astonishment.

'Come on now, Tilly,' interjected Matt. 'You go and get dressed and I'll come and give you a hand in a minute. Then we'll have breakfast.'

'Okay!' Tilly shouted as she dashed off to her room. 'I will shut the door so you can't see me,' she added.

'Oh, she's delightful, Matt,' said Sophie.

'Yeah, she's a sweetheart. Did you manage to sleep at all?'

'Not much. My mind was too full. Strange isn't it. When I did wake up, I thought, great, going to see my dad today and then I remembered. It all seems so unreal. Even with that policeman – not that I want to ever see him again. You know, you think things are okay and then suddenly they're not. I've never lost someone close – by death, I mean – is that all normal?'

'Absolutely, Sophie.' Matt replied reassuringly. 'It takes a while. That whole air of disbelief and hoping it'll turn out to be a bad dream. It's important to be gentle with yourself.'

'Yeah. I'm not good at that,' said the nurse who cared deeply for her patients but not for herself. 'Shall I make some tea?'

The morning passed slowly. Playing with Tilly provided helpful distraction while Matt dealt with the washing and other Saturday morning domesticity.

'It's good you've talked to Tilly about Jo a bit, Matt,' Sophie said at one point.

'Yes, gently does it really,' he replied. 'Obviously, I haven't said anything about what actually happened and probably won't for a very long time. I think she knows Jo is in a better place and we'll often look at the photo together,' he nodded in the direction of the computer. 'And I've got some others on my phone. She likes seeing the ones of her as a baby. It's sweet, she'll often say night, night to the photo when she goes to bed. We say a prayer at bedtime and ask God to look after Mummy, that type of thing.'

'Mummy's in her happy place,' said Tilly as she played with her toys on the floor.

'That's right, love, she is,' her dad replied.

'Take care through these next two or three weeks,' Matt said, as Sophie got ready to leave. 'There'll be a lot to do and to process. And after that – well that can be difficult too when you're trying to get back into normal routines again. I'm afraid many people tend to lose interest once the funeral is over,' he added with a tinge of sadness borne from his own experience.

'Umm... yeah. Thanks,' Sophie replied. 'Oh, while I remember, I was thinking about it in the night. Because you are still technically a patient – although Steve sees you, the overall responsibility falls to me. I'll need to tell my boss what's happened: nursing code of conduct and all that. Is that okay with you?'

'Of course, I hope you don't get in to trouble.'

'It should be okay. Jane's pretty sensible and if I tell her straight away it's probably best. I'm on leave now for a week so I'll email her from my sister's to let her know and then it's in writing rather some garbled phone call. Rosie works in human resources so she can help me phrase it. Anyway, I best be off. I'll text you later.'

Picking up her bag, she gave Matt a kiss on the cheek and their hands touched for a moment.

'Don't I get a kiss?' demanded Tilly.

'Of course you do, Tilly,' replied Sophie. 'And a hug too.'

CHAPTER 5

We can all start again

Hi Matt, thanks again for earlier. It's been good to see Rosie. I'm going to stay here for a couple of nights & we can get other things moving on Mon. Will be in touch. S x

Matt was pleased to hear from Sophie that evening.

Thanks, that's good. Been thinking of you & let me know if I can do anything. M x

He wasn't sure whether to end with a kiss but she had, so thought it would be okay. He'd been taken aback by how Sophie's loss had brought up so much from deep within him. Memories of Jo. Her love and her loss. The accident. The change in who he was. It was over eighteen months now and yet it seemed as if it was only yesterday. It was hard to accept he wasn't 'over it' as much as thought he was or pretended to be.

Not being able to go to Jo's funeral had left all sorts of mixed emotions and scars. It was good Will Taylor did what he did although it wasn't the same as doing it himself. It wasn't as if it was easy to visit the grave at the same Cotswold church where they married either. He hoped one day he could. A day to finally say goodbye.

Tilly had found him crying earlier that afternoon. 'Sophie's Daddy looks after Mummy now,' she said, bringing him a pretend cup of tea and her favourite cuddly toy, Clara the camel. 'Don't worry about a thing' she sang: Bob Marley would have liked it and so did Matt.

It was the first time he'd cried for while. Music would sometimes do it, as would seeing someone who looked like Jo. Dreams about her were lovely except when he woke up and realised she wasn't there. It helped having a novel on the go. Something to be absorbed by – especially at night when other thoughts took control (as they usually did). It was easy to forget that most of his characters weren't real people: they became a source of comfort in themselves. He wished he could meet them.

Matt sometimes wondered if he should have been angry with Greg. Would it have been cathartic? Why didn't Greg do anything to avoid hitting them? Why have I been left like this: widowed, and with half a useless body? Why did you let it all happen, God? He remembered his counsellor saying such feelings may go on for a long time and that it was natural and normal. 'Grief isn't something that can be switched on and off like a tap,' he told him. 'Sometimes it'll switch on all by itself.'

'Oh, Jo, I wish you were here,' he said to her photo that evening, taking it off the desk and holding it against his chest. He slept with it that night.

■　■　■

Sophie had daily contact with Matt while she was at Rosie's: mainly by text. Sometimes long interchanges. Sometimes short. In the end, Sophie spent most of her week's leave with her sister. She said it was good to have time there and to see her twin nephew and niece too. They were seven now. Rosie's husband, Paul was an architect in a small firm working on new office blocks in London. The two of them were in the early stages of getting planning permission for a self-build as their current house was too small for growing children and a dog.

Sophie went back to work after her holiday and then took another couple of days off for the funeral. It was touching how many people came to the crematorium, Sophie texted Matt afterwards. Several people from her dad's former workplace went as did a few from the social club he used to frequent before he became too unwell to go there safely.

People at work were really kind when they heard about Dad. A couple gave me 'told you so' eyebrows when they heard about the other thing. Jane was fine & we had a good chat. Sorry I've not been able to call in: will you be around on Sat? S x

Sat in the park that Saturday afternoon, Sophie reflected on all that had happened and talked about the funeral and the time with her sister. 'Rosie told me something I never knew before. She didn't think it was Dad's dementia talking, but it seems there were some really bad arguments between him and Mum when we were very young. Things getting thrown about, that type of thing. Apparently Social Services got involved and threatened to take the two of us away. It was then that Mum left and Dad was able to convince them he could look after us. I don't remember any of that – I was only two when she left and even Rosie said she didn't have much recollection of it even though she was five. With Dad out working, I grew up seeing my grandparents a lot. They're still alive – both in their eighties and pretty frail. They live a long way away and couldn't make the funeral, which was difficult for them. We speak on the phone every five or six weeks although it's a couple of years since I last saw them. They're really sweet. Grandad's a scream.'

'Have you ever met your mum?' Matt asked.

'No. I don't remember her at all. I've seen a photo of her with me just after I was born and a couple of others when I was a bit older. Dad refused to talk about her so we learnt not to ask. Rosie's always been the more sensible of the two of us and she became "mum" in many ways. I didn't know any different. As I got older, I knew that other people's home lives weren't like ours but, there again, loads of kids at school only had one parent at home so that was just how it was. I'm glad Dad did talk about it in the end. It's good to know a bit more – and to understand why he once told me he'd never get married again.

'So, I guess that explains partly why I've always felt insecure and tried to find happiness and everything through my job and… well, you know... men. All in all, life's been a case of trial and error,' she laughed. 'Most of it a trial and an awful lot of error.' (That's a good line for my book, thought Matt.)

'We can all start again, Sophie,' he said, realising it sounded a bit trite.

'Really?' Sophie looked at Matt, not sure if she believed him. 'Well, I guess you know that more than many,' she conceded. 'I mean… is it okay to ask you about Jo?'

'It is for you, Sophie.'

'I've never experienced what you two had, you know. I guess I've always just rushed into relationships and never really thought about them. You seemed to have had something special.'

'Yeah, we did.' Matt smiled. 'I think it helped that we became good friends first. It was a while before we started going out. She'd had a bad experience in the first year at uni and was hesitant about committing to a relationship – despite all the admirers she had. She was far more dedicated to studying than I was too. It was a shock to both of us when I got a First and hers was a 2.1. She was robbed, mate,' he added with a cockney accent.

'Obviously, our shared faith was really important and it shaped who we were together and the way we tried to relate to each other. Didn't always get it right, of course. We had noisy and silent arguments like lots of people. We both knew fairly early on, though, that we might get married but we didn't want to rush things. Then there were all the practicalities. Leaving uni, getting jobs, going out into the big wide world and finding our own places to live etcetera.'

'You didn't live together, then?' asked Sophie, finding it hard to hide her surprise (she'd had two such ventures – both short-lived).

'No, we didn't even sleep together.'

'Really?' Her surprise now fully revealed.

'Yeah. That bit was tough, I have to say,' Matt smiled. 'It was a lifestyle choice in many ways. We really wanted to save it for our wedding night.'

They sat watching the ducks on the river.

'Shall we get a coffee?' Matt asked.

'Hug first?'

■　■　■

Sophie went round to Matt and Tilly's most Saturdays after that. Sometimes the three of them would go down by the river or to the park. Tilly would feed the ducks or go in the play area. Occasionally, they'd bump into Greg and Ian. Greg had finally been able to return to work part-time. Unusually for a solo sweeper, he was working with two others on the High Street/Minster round which was a busy public area: just in case anything happened. The banter had returned – and he'd even started to read Matt's book. Ian and Greg had decided to enter into a civil partnership so were busy planning their big day. They hinted at sending invitations to both Matt and Sophie but there were already over a hundred on the 'possibles list' so couldn't promise anything. Sophie and Matt felt it was good to see them both moving on.

Other weekends, they'd stay indoors, playing with Tilly and then watch something on Netflix in the evenings. It was good for all of them. Mutual stability on the rollercoaster of grief.

Although the wheelchair remained his constant companion, Matt gained more confidence in those spring and summer months, even managing a few steps around the flat with the aid of crutches. Using dumbbells and doing his upper body exercises complemented the gentler ones for his legs. He'd like to think that in a year's time he'd complete what he now called the Flat Race: from South Sofa to Bathroom Bridge. The prospect of walking outside seemed like rowing the Atlantic, though: he felt safe in his sheltered mooring.

Like the previous one, the anniversary of Jo's death was a tough day. Sophie went over to Matt's in her lunch break again. She hadn't seen him cry so deeply and for so long.

Two years had the same impact as if it had been only two days. She went back in the evening to make sure he was okay: he was. He'd even bought a quiche and put together a salad. 'The work of my own fair hands, Sophie – not even touched the microwave,' he joked. Tilly didn't like the lettuce but loved the ice cream for afters.

■ ■ ■

Matt finished working at the pound shop when Tilly started pre-school at the beginning of September. It was only a ten-minute push to the same site as the primary school she'd go to in a year's time. Continuing to write his second novel involved a lot of online research, but the storyline was gradually coming together and the word count was increasing. He also began doing some admin work for his dad's church for which they paid him the National Living Wage. It was good to draw on his design skills and improve the publicity and the website for the community centre.

In the same month, as a way of improving her career prospects, Sophie started a part-time Masters Degree and she also got a new boss at work. Jane Wilson had left suddenly to do 'project work' but no one knew anything more. The new manager, Mrs Farquharson as she insisted on people calling her, was a stickler and beginning to make Sophie's life difficult. Others told her not to take it personally but Sophie believed it might be.

Not being a party animal, Matt celebrated his 30th by having lunch with his mum and dad. Thanks to a rather unusual and eminently practical gift from them, he now had a car seat so they could take Tilly out more easily in Sophie's aging Nissan Almera.

'I've got my chair. You've got your chair,' Tilly commented on this tangible demonstration of 21st Century equality.

With that in place, Sophie joined them after work. The warm, late September afternoon sun made for a lovely birthday tea on the beach. Two ice creams later and after digging all the way to Australia, Tilly slept most of the way home. A bedtime story from Sophie provided a happy end to her day too. Tilly always liked Sophie's made-up stories about Clara the Camel and all the adventures and scrapes she got into with her other cuddly friends.

'How's the book going?' Sophie asked as they finished off the washing up. Matt had perfected the art of leaning against the sink and wiping up at the same time.

'Yeah, it's coming along okay, thanks,' he replied. 'Easier now Tilly's started pre-school. I can do the writing alongside the work for Dad. My publisher's been really good and they extended the deadline in light of what's happened. One of the hardest bits is constantly going over the text and editing and proofreading and all that. It's so hard to pick up mistakes in my own typing.'

'It's a sequel to the first one, right?' Sophie asked.

'Yes, it's moved on from the fifties with people like Rosa Parks and the bus boycotts in Montgomery, Alabama, to the Martin Luther King years: what a man he was, Sophie.'

'Is it the same protagonist?'

'Now that's a proper writer's word,' joked Matt. Sophie splashed water into his face. Matt stretched the tea towel and launched it like a catapult. It fell on the floor. 'Serves you right,' joked Sophie as she picked it up for him. The looked at each other. Their eyes lingered. Their eyes spoke.

'Yeah, he's very much involved in the whole non-violent protest scene with MLK. He's there at the Lincoln Memorial too. Everyone knows about the "I have a dream" speech but there was so much more. So many other speeches that day and people like Mahalia Jackson, the amazing gospel singer was there too. You know it was her who urged him to include the bit about the dream – so on the day he just improvised. Wow! A quarter of a million people were there – and most of them didn't hear it because someone had sabotaged the P.A.'

'Any love interest? The first book had a fairly, umm, raunchy bit in it, didn't it?' she teased.

'Oh, so you've read it!' Matt laughed. The atmosphere was changing. 'Yeah, of course. I mean, the lead character – the protagonist, as you called him,' he said in a posh, literary voice. 'Well, he's a good-looking guy. Thirty years old. Been through some tough times. And he really likes a beautiful blonde-haired nurse who's become a really good friend. But... he doesn't know if she feels the same way and he doesn't want to risk losing her friendship by saying the wrong thing.'

'And she's,' interjected Sophie, 'had a string of failed relationships and doesn't know if she can take the risk again – but wants to feel as if perhaps she can?'

'That's about it, Sophie. I'm a bit stuck there. Don't quite know where it's going next.'

'Do you think he might like to kiss her?'

'Umm. Yes, I like that idea. I think he would, Sophie. I think he would.'

So they did.

'Well, it's about time!' shouted Tilly, emerging from the bathroom. 'Nite Nite!' she grinned.

They stood laughing.

They stood holding.

They stood together.

■　■　■

As Sophie drove home that night, she reflected on how many times she wouldn't have made that journey. How a kiss would have led to much more straight away. This time, she hadn't wanted that. She felt happy and excited, and even more than that, she felt safe and peaceful. This was different and she liked it.

Matt sat on the sofa. Going over in his head what had happened. There were times when he thought he'd never kiss again – let alone love again. It was a heady mix of emotions. He didn't know whether to laugh or cry. He looked at the photo. 'Is that okay with you, Jo?' he asked as the needle touched vinyl at thirty-three and a third. The music played once more.

■　■　■

Giving themselves a couple of weeks to get to used to it, Matt and Sophie kept this change in their relationship quiet. Midweek texts and weekend visits continued, supplemented by Sophie calling in when work allowed. Matt was conscious she always had to come to his place (Sophie's first floor flat had no lift to it). They enjoyed being with each other in a different and more intimate way. A comfortable sense that this was the right time to be moving on. They both found it hard to concentrate on work, however. New love's distraction was very, very distracting.

Whenever they made it public, they both knew they would each have to have difficult conversations. Professional ethics dictated Sophie needed to tell her new manager, who she was struggling to get on with (the feeling was mutual). Matt thought his parents would be fine – indeed, probably delighted – but he was concerned about how Jo's mum and dad may react. They still visited him every four or five weeks. He'd learnt to take them as he found them, although last time they seemed particularly distant even though they didn't allude to anything. Something was going on and he didn't know what it was.

Des and Janice arrived one Sunday tea-time to look after Tilly while Sophie and Matt went to church. Their granddaughter immediately climbed on to Matt's lap and announced: 'I saw Daddy and Sophie having a kissy-wissy in the kitchen.'

Sophie went bright red. 'Tilly!' Matt said exasperatingly, trying to control his laughter at the same time.

Janice's eyes opened wide, an action quickly imitated by her mouth: 'Do you have something to tell us, young man and young lady?'

Standing beside Matt, Sophie turned away in embarrassment. Matt reached out his hand and she put hers into it.

'Are you two courtin'?' she probed further.

'Yes, Mum, we're courtin'.'

'Well, come to Mama, Sophie Howlett,' she said, opening her arms wide and holding Sophie's head to her bosom. 'You know, I kept saying to Desmond that I thought something was going on: I told him in no uncertain terms that he wasn't to say anything.'

'It's only been two weeks, Mum,' explained Matt. 'And please keep it to yourselves, would you? We don't want those tongues wagging too much at the moment.'

'Why, of course, man,' replied Des. 'I won't put it in the notices until next Sunday.' They all laughed and gathered in a hug encircling Matt and Tilly.

'Jo would be pleased, Matt,' Des said as they stood there.

'Thanks. I'm glad you think so. That means a lot,' Matt replied. 'We'd appreciate your thoughts tomorrow, though. I'm going to FaceTime Rob and Gill and tell them and Sophie's going to explain to her boss.'

'I thought you weren't a patient anymore, Matt?' said Janice.

'No, he's not,' replied Sophie. 'Nurses have a code of conduct around relationships with former patients so I just want to be open about it.'

'Just like with us social workers, Sophie. You take care in that, won't you? Make sure they don't turn it against you,' advised Janice. 'Oh, this is such good news, you two.

You've both been through such a lot and I am so glad you took your time about it. Making sure you both feel ready. You know, Des and I…'

'I think we'll leave our story until another time shall we, Janice?' interrupted Des. 'Your mother was worth the long wait though,' he added.

'Desmond!'

CHAPTER 6

Suspended

Matt spent hours rehearsing what he was going to say to Jo's parents and worrying about how they might react. Even though it was now over two years on, they, like him, had not fully come to terms with their loss. Seeing them on screen, Matt could tell things weren't right. Gill had been crying and Rob looked strained. They passed through the usual pleasantries, catching up about Tilly and how she was getting on at pre-school and talking about the McKenzies' allotment.

There was a pause. 'I've got something to tell you,' said Gill and Matt simultaneously. Matt smiled. 'You first,' he said.

'It's not good news, I'm afraid, Matt,' Gill said. 'Jo's sister, Penny, has cancer.'

Matt didn't know what to say. Words would have failed to express his reaction in any case. Gill talked about what had happened and how Penny discovered a lump on her breast. They were relieved that Penny sought help straight away and the doctors were hopeful of a complete recovery as she was responding well to treatment. All the same, the thought of possibly losing a second child had ripped apart what was left of their world.

'Why do bad things happen to good people?' Matt thought to himself.

'So, what is it you wanted to tell us, Matt?' asked Rob after the conversation had run its inevitable stuttering course.

Suddenly it all seemed irrelevant. 'Oh, it can wait, you've got far too much on your plate,' Matt replied, albeit knowing it was relevant to both him and them.

'Is it good news, Matt? We could do with some good news,' said Gill.

Matt smiled. 'It is for me and I hope you will be pleased too.'

'You've found someone?' Gill said, helping Matt avoid any further awkwardness. She smiled for the first time in the conversation. Matt took the smile as an encouragement to tell them about Sophie. He needn't have worried, after all.

'Oh, that is good news, Matt,' said Gill after they'd heard all about her. 'I think we may have been there once when she visited you in hospital, if I'm thinking of the right person.'

'Thanks for telling us, Matt' said Rob encouragingly, 'That can't have been easy for you. I expect you were wondering how we might react? We've often thought it would be nice for you to meet someone else and for Tilly too, of course. You're a great lad. You'll always be our son-in-law and we're sure Jo would be happy for you too.'

Matt struggled to hold back the tears. That meant even more than when his dad said the same.

■ ■ ■

Matt's phone rang later that morning. Sophie. It was a bad signal. She was in floods of tears and he couldn't tell what she was saying. Amidst all the surrounding noise and interference, he picked out the words 'horrible' and 'suspended'.

'Love you,' he said, as she rang off.

Thirty minutes later, Sophie was sat with Matt's arm around her. Music played softly in the background, providing warmth and stillness, as she told him about what had happened.

Sophie had already planned to see Joan Farquharson that afternoon but on arriving at work was immediately called in to her office.

'We need to talk,' commanded the manager. Wielding her power further, she then disappeared for a few minutes returning with an advisor from HR. He was new, young and inexperienced: Joan Farquharson had asked for him specifically.

'I gather you've been seeing a former patient, Nurse Howlett. Do you want to tell us about it.' It was an instruction not a question.

Joan Farquharson sat staring at Sophie. She was in her early fifties and dressed in a way that would not have been out of place on Real Housewives. Sophie already knew her manager's personality was not as attractive as her appearance. She'd come across many in management who tried to throw their weight around (an attribute which particularly suited Joan Farquharson). Sophie thought it sad that some female managers feel they have to imitate the worst traits of their male counterparts in order to prove they're good enough.

Managing to stay professional and calm, Sophie told them about what happened at the beginning of the year, the email she'd sent Jane Wilson at the time and their subsequent conversation, and how the patient was discharged shortly afterwards.

'And you've continued to see him?' Joan Farquharson asked accusingly. Sophie acknowledged she had and pointed out that Jane also knew that. 'You say it was a platonic relationship?' she emphasised with an underlining sneer. 'I find that difficult to believe. You have, so I understand, shall we say, a reputation… something about a fight with a policeman over a pizza, I gather.' She laughed, looking at her audience for approval.

The HR advisor shuffled uncomfortably in his seat. He kept his eyes firmly on Sophie when really he wanted to stare at Joan Farquharson. Sophie looked to him for support but nothing came back.

Remaining calm was becoming more difficult: 'If you are trying to insinuate that it was or is a sexual relationship with Mr West then no, it is not. And,' Sophie was getting in to her stride, 'the incident you refer to was nothing to do with anyone here. It was not over a pizza,' she said emphatically. 'If you must know, it was about that person's use of pornographic images.' Sophie paused for effect –

she could play the game too. 'He would have injured me – in fact, he did injure me – and it would have been worse had I not defended myself.

'And that same evening,' Sophie continued, determined to set the record straight. 'That same evening, as you know from the email you have in front of you, my dad died and because I had no one else to turn to I went to Mr West for support.'

She could feel her voice breaking and her eyes moistening. Quickly regaining control, she continued: 'I do know that was unethical but I hope you will also agree that my action of emailing Jane the very next day was to recognise how the situation could be misinterpreted by other people.' (She resisted the urge to add 'As you have done.')

Before Joan Farquharson could accuse her of having admitted the offence with which she was being charged, Sophie asked. 'So why may I ask has this been brought up now, ten months on?'

The young man spoke at last: 'Unfortunately, under the policies, Jane should have passed on your email and a report of the conversation to HR straight away. This has only recently come to light and because it was a potential breach of the Nursing Code of Conduct, we will need to investigate further.'

'So that's why Jane was moved on,' Sophie thought to herself. 'Calling it "project work" is always a good way of hiding things from other people.'

'Are you still seeing Mr West?' the HR man asked. His more conciliatory tone enabled Sophie to calm her anger but, recalling Janice's comment, she also wondered if they were playing good cop, bad cop.

'I am,' she replied. 'In fact, in order to respect the Code of Conduct I was going to see Mrs Farquharson later today in order to tell her that Mr West and I are now in a relationship and have been for the last two weeks. We are not living together and have no plans to do so.'

'You know that having a relationship with a former patient could be seen as breaching the Code of Conduct?' her manager said, pleased at the possibility of another offence being taken into consideration.

'I am,' replied Sophie. 'At the same time, he has not been a patient for eight months.'

Sophie cried as Matt held her in his arms. 'Then they asked me to sit outside,' she continued. 'In a corridor, for goodness' sake, with people going backwards and forwards making jokes about being outside the Headteacher's study. Twenty minutes later and I was called back in and told that a formal investigation would take place and that I was suspended on full pay until further notice. And then there was the humiliation of Farquharson taking me back to my office to pick up my bag and coat, and in front of everyone else, escorting me out of the building. She must have really enjoyed that,' Sophie reflected bitterly.

'I'm sorry, Matt. It's all my fault,' she said, wiping her eyes. 'I could lose my job over this and that's not fair on you. I love you but maybe it's not the right thing. I've told you before I'm no good at this. I'm not good enough for you, Matt.'

For the second time that day, words failed him as he fought hard to resist the surge of emotions that rose to the surface. The knight in shining armour rushing to rescue his fair maiden. The cowering soldier being attacked by memories of love and loss.

'Sophie, we've been through a lot already and this is one other thing,' he said, keeping his inner turmoil at bay.

'Seems to me you've been treated really badly: you did the right thing by telling them,' he said reassuringly. 'Look, you've been there for me and I will be here for you. We'll get through this – whatever the outcome, it won't make any difference to how I feel about you. It's you, Sophie, I love, not the nurse.' He felt his words were all rather trite but saying anything without lots of cliches was temporarily beyond him.

'Thank you. Love you too.' They sat silently. There was a comfort in the silence. The music played on. Coldplay's X&Y album. Track four. Matt didn't know if he could fix it.

'I'm not allowed to have contact with anyone at work and they said the investigation will take a couple of weeks,' Sophie continued after a few minutes. 'They may want to talk to you as part of it… sorry. How did it go with Jo's parents?' she said, moving the subject on.

'Oh, Matt,' Sophie said after hearing about Jo's sister. 'What on earth is going on?'

He'd struggled with that question many times over the last two and a bit years. 'At this precise moment, love, I don't know,' he admitted.

The intercom buzzed. Tilly's return from pre-school provided a welcome lift out of the hole they'd found themselves in. Des stayed long enough to hear a résumé of events and for all of them to look at the paintings his granddaughter had done.

■ ■ ■

The two-week long investigation became four and Sophie spent a lot of them at Matt's. They often worked together: Matt at his desk, Sophie on the settee with her laptop working on her Masters. It helped both of them mentally, spiritually and physically. Although there were times when the strain showed – they once had a tiff over the fact Matt had put washing on the sofa because there wasn't anywhere else. They soon learnt there was nothing that making up afterwards couldn't resolve.

The time off work gave Sophie unexpected and much needed space for herself and the capacity to think about her career. She was losing her previously strong sense of vocation. She'd not been happy in the managerial role and missed the hands-on contact with patients (apart from with Matt, that is). Sophie knew the worst that could happen would be to be dismissed and struck off, although her Royal College of Nursing representative thought it unlikely they'd go that far. As those strange weeks went by, with her confidence dented and security unlocked, there were some dark and difficult days. Throughout it all, though, Sophie had an unexpected, inner sense of peace. Even if it had started with an error of professional judgment, she felt she would be stronger by the end.

Supported by her RCN rep, Sophie endured a long, intrusive interview with the investigating manager. Matt's had been shorter but still personal: he got the impression the investigator didn't quite understand what all the fuss was about.

Matt joked with Sophie afterwards: 'You should have seen his face when he first saw me. I mean, he hadn't expected to be met by someone in a wheelchair. And when he saw the wedding photo on the wall, he looked totally bewildered!' Matt impersonated his Welsh accent to a tee: '"You are Mister Maa-thew West, aren't you? And this is about Nurse Howl-ett?"'

The subsequent disciplinary hearing had the air of a courtroom drama. On one side of a large table, as stony faced as Mount Rushmore, sat Joan Farquharson. Also present were a couple of HR people, the investigating manager and the union rep. Sophie sat there too. She knew in her heart she had breached the principle of the Code of

Conduct, but also had the clear conviction of having done the right things to try and make amends.

The Chair of the panel listened as reports were presented and questions were asked and answered. After a gruelling hour and a quarter, a prolonged adjournment was spent in a windowless side room. There was nothing more to be done.

Forty minutes later, they all returned to the meeting room and, sitting like judge, jury and executioner rolled into one, the Chairman read out his verdict: 'Having read through the evidence and reports, and heard each of the further statements today, it is my opinion that Nurse Howlett's behaviour in January did breach the Nursing Code of Conduct.'

The turning of Sophie's stomach synchronised with Joan Farquharson's nodding head. 'However,' he added, 'there are significant mitigating circumstances. It is clear that Nurse Howlett informed her original manager, Jane Wilson, as soon as was practically possible. I am also satisfied that Nurse Howlett showed good intent to inform her current manager about the subsequent change in the relationship with Mr West.' He looked up from his script. 'An interchange that could have been handled more sensitively,' he said pointedly in the direction of Sophie's manager. 'I am also satisfied that Mr West was not subject to any abuse of clinical power by Nurse Howlett and that he entered into the personal friendship willingly.'

A noisy slurp from Joan Farquharson's glass of water provided a sign of her disapproval.

'Nurse Howlett,' the Chair continued, 'you did breach the Code of Conduct. However, under the circumstances I have decided not to recommend any further disciplinary action beyond this hearing. You will, however, be given a final written warning which will remain on your file for twelve months. Any further breach of professional standards in that time may result in dismissal on grounds of gross misconduct. You are no longer suspended from work and may return immediately.' Lifting his head, he looked directly at Sophie: 'Although I appreciate you may not wish to do so today.'

Sophie loosened her grip on the small wooden cross that Matt had given her. 'Thank you,' she said.

A crack appeared in the stony face. It wouldn't be long before there was a complete landslide.

■ ■ ■

A week after they had celebrated the outcome with a meal out, Sophie arrived at Matt's one cold, early December evening. 'You are not going to believe this, Matt West,' she exclaimed as she walked in. 'Jane Wilson has come back, which is wonderful. And the old cow… well, she's gone. Completely. Dismissed for gross misconduct. Seems… get this… seems she's been in a relationship – a sexual relationship, I'll have you know… with a current patient! Not the first time either. Her previous marriage was to a former one. Talk about hypocrisy!'

Justice was done and justice was seen to be done.

CHAPTER 7

Tilly asks a question

Matt had spent half an hour looking out of the window waiting for Sophie to arrive. They hadn't seen each other since before Christmas and he'd not felt so excited since waiting for Jo on their wedding day. He'd really missed Sophie and amidst all the anticipation of her arrival, worried in case she didn't want to see him anymore. The loss of confidence was still a shadow hanging over him.

The journey to Matt's flat took an age. All the lights were red as Sophie drove through the rush hour traffic that first Friday afternoon of the New Year. The butterflies in her stomach danced in excitement. She wanted seeing him to feel the same as it had the last time they were together.

It was Tilly who grabbed the first hug. 'Come and see what I got for Christmas,' she said pulling Sophie off to her bedroom. They looked and they smiled. 'Love you,' mouthed Matt. 'Love you, too,' replied Sophie, forming her fingers into a heart. 'I guess I'll see you in a few minutes!' she added. 'Fish fingers okay?' asked Matt. 'Chips!' shouted Tilly.

Over tea, they talked about all that had happened since they were last together. Missing her dad at Christmas had been difficult for Sophie and it had been good to spend most of the festive season with Rosie and family. The Masters was going well and Sophie had looked at job adverts every so often. There was nothing local which attracted her, although she knew that was normal for the time of year.

Tilly had been a sheep in the pre-school Nativity Play and Matt observed how unusual it was to see Darth Vader, Superman and Elsa visiting the Baby Jesus before the Wise Men got there. Now three and a half, Tilly had been more excited this year than ever before. It had been a long time since Matt had seen five o'clock in the morning. The build up to Christmas had been busy with work for his dad's church, although he'd managed to do some writing for his second novel between shopping for presents.

The good news from the McKenzies was that Penny's situation was not nearly as bad as they'd feared and she'd being given the all clear for the time-being. On Christmas Day, Des announced he was planning to move on from being at the church. Janice had also decided to finish work so the two of them could spend more time together. Both nearly sixty, and both in good health, they hoped it would give them time to so do something they had thought about for many years.

After a final chip wiped up the last bit of ketchup, Tilly dipped her spoon in to chocolate ice cream. 'Sophie,' she said, sucking with a noisy slurp. 'Are you going to be my Mummy?'

Sophie looked at Matt. Matt smiled. 'Well, Tilly, that's your…' Sophie began to reply, as she looked over at Matt's computer. 'Oh, where's the photo gone, Tilly?'

'It's in my bedroom,' she replied.

'I'll explain later,' said Matt.

'Well, the lady in the photo is your Mummy, Tilly.'

'I know that, silly.' She giggled. 'Oh. Tilly, Silly. Silly. Tilly. Are you going to be my Mummy? Are you going to marry Daddy?'

Matt and Sophie looked at each other, laughing embarrassed laughs.

'Oh, Tilly. You do ask the most wonderful questions,' replied Matt. 'Have you finished?' he added, quickly moving the conversation on.

'Yummy!' she said, the taste of the final spoonful overwhelming any lasting desire to know the answer.

With Tilly bathed and another episode of Clara the Camel adventures told, Sophie and Matt could finally sit down together at South Sofa. 'Lovely to be with you again,' Sophie said. Matt agreed as he put his arm around her.

'Matt, you know I've been looking at other jobs? Well, there's been nothing much that fits my experience and qualifications but before Christmas I saw an ad from a charity which runs a rehab centre for people who have spinal injuries. They want a Senior Rehabilitation Nurse. They're doing all sorts of new experimental work and it would fit really well with my Masters. The closing date isn't until mid-February and it sounds like a really good job.'

'Yeah, it does, Sophie,' replied Matt, noticing how her voice didn't quite match the enthusiasm of her words. 'Just up your street,' trying not to make his reply likewise. 'Are you going to apply?'

'Well, I tried to dismiss it when I first saw the advert, to be honest, but it's niggled away in me. I don't know if it's the right time.' She paused. 'Anyway, I phoned them today to find out a bit more. You know, one of those "informal conversation" things and well, they were really positive about my experience and all that. I mean, really positive. They've invited me to visit next week and have a look around.' She took a sharp intake of breath. 'There's a but, Matt. A very big but. It's 250 miles away.'

Matt felt his stomach turn over.

'I don't know what to do, Matt. I want to be with you and yet it looks like a really good job,' she said, realising she was trying to talk herself out of it and into it all at the same time. 'And you know, jobwise, I've had itchy feet for a while really. I'm looking to move on.'

First his stomach, now his heart. Matt's chest tightened as Sophie continued speaking. His mind thrown back to that fateful June evening. A vivid picture of Jo speaking those words like a forty-five played at thirty-three and a third.

'Matt? Matt! Are you listening?' Sophie's frustration at his inattention broke in to his anxious thoughts. 'This is important, Matt. I really want to talk to you about it.'

A single tear emerged from his left eye. Sophie put her hand in his. 'Oh, Matt. What's wrong?'

'Sorry, Sophie. It's just... I've never told anyone this – anyone at all. That phrase you used. You weren't to know. "I'm looking to move on." They were Jo's last words.'

Sophie held him as the tears poured out the pain of resurgent memories.

After a coffee and leftover Christmas cake, it was Matt who picked up the topic. 'It does sound a good job, Sophie. Is there something else stopping you?' he asked, feeling there may be.

'Yeah,' she replied. 'I'm scared of having a long-distance relationship. I got burnt once. It was him who moved and it was okay to begin with... and then good old Sophie Howlett decided to pay him a surprise visit and...'

'There was someone else?' Matt completed her sentence.

They sat in silence for a moment. Hands stroking hands.

'It's also what Tilly said, to be honest,' Sophie said with a smile. 'You know?'

'Yes, I know. I've been thinking about that as well – all over Christmas,' Matt replied, with a laugh. 'That's partly why I moved the photo. Tilly draws comfort from it now she's becoming a bit more aware of her situation being different to other kids. I will never forget Jo and you know that. I so appreciate you accept that Jo is and always will be part of my life. I love you, Sophie, and want to be with you too. And,' he never thought he would use the phrase for himself, 'I'm looking to move on as well and I didn't want you to feel that having the photo there meant you were… less important.'

Sophie gripped Matt's hand. 'You needn't have done that, you know – I was actually fine with it. That's very thoughtful of you.' They kissed.

'So what do I do about this job, Matt?' she said, curling up her legs as she leant against him. 'I mean what if I went and I really liked it?'

'Then you could apply.'

'And what if I got it?'

Matt laughed. 'Yeah, I know. It's all the what ifs, isn't it?

'Well, if it's okay with you, I guess I could visit them and see what happens? But I want to be here with you too!' She laughed. She cried.

'Look, I don't want you to be living 250 miles away, Sophie.' Matt's arms held her tightly. 'I want the best for you. If it was the right job then we take it from there. I wouldn't want you to be stuck here in six months' time thinking "Oh, I wish I'd applied for it." There's no harm in visiting, love. It doesn't commit you to anything.'

■ ■ ■

Matt's parents came over to see him on the day Sophie went on the visit. 'We've got something we want to talk to you about,' they'd said in a phone conversation a few days previously. Matt wanted to give them an update too.

'So, there you have it,' said Matt, after he'd told them more about Sophie's job dilemma (albeit not mentioning Tilly's question).

'It will become clear, Matt,' said Des reassuringly. 'Sometimes we have to wait. Sometimes we have to step out in faith and see what happens. Not always easy though, is it?'

Matt nodded. 'So, what is it you wanted to talk to me about?'

'Well,' said Des, 'we've been thinking about what to do next. For a long time now, in fact ever since we lost your brother, David, all those years ago, your Mum and I have had an idea of offering something for people who are bereaved. And since then, of course, we've both lost both our parents and you lost Jo.'

'We lost Jo too,' Janice added.

'And you lost something of me,' said Matt.

Des and Janice looked at each other, slightly taken aback by their son's unexpected but accurate insight. 'Yes, that's right, Matt, we did. But you're still Matt – and we've seen new things in you also, you know,' Des said. 'I see people every week who have lost someone. What with funerals and anniversaries. And in many ways, it's been Jo's death that has made us think about it all again.'

'Initially, it sounded a bit crazy,' Janice continued. 'However, something's happened that may make it possible. We want to open a place that would offer a safe haven for people who are grieving.'

'A place where people can come and stay,' Des added. 'Where we could offer limited counselling, prayer support, good meals, comfortable rooms for people to have a short stay and available for anyone, any loss, any timescale. You know, people who have just lost someone or perhaps, like us, lost someone a long, long time ago and have never fully come to terms with it. People who are looking to move on.'

That phrase again. Matt began to fully realise the depth of his parents' own loss. David had died aged four from meningitis when Matt was just two. What pain they had carried in the years since then. He thought of Rob and Gill McKenzie too, and Sophie.

'You know Thomas Southcott, don't you, Matt?' asked Janice.

'What, the chap at church who owns the hotel on the edge of town?'

'That's him,' she continued. 'Well, he's thinking of closing down. He's not well and it's hard work keeping that business running and managing a team of staff and with guests coming and going all the time.'

'Lovely setting though with all that parkland,' Matt observed.

'Yes and there's twelve rooms and live-in accommodation for about four staff,' replied Des. 'Thomas doesn't want to see it go to a developer and become even more new houses. So what he's done – and this is where it gets both exciting and scary – is he's offered it to us.'

'We had talked to him about all this in the past,' explained Janice. 'And then he came to us a couple of weeks ago and he'd been to see his solicitor and said that if we formed a charity he would effectively donate the hotel. He owns it outright and doesn't have any family to leave it to. He even said he would give us enough money to pay a year's salary for the cook if we wanted her to stay on.'

'So, we think that if we could raise money to pay for some alterations and employ a couple of housekeeping staff,' Des continued. 'Then people who come to it would pay for meals and any professional support we needed to buy in. And the rest would be run on donations. We'd ask people to give what they feel they can.'

'And I guess that now I'm more settled and Tilly's not with you so much that you've, well, not got those extra demands going on as much as they were,' Matt observed.

'Yes, that's right, Matt,' replied Janice. 'It seems the right time and we're still young enough and healthy enough to do something else with our lives. We've got a lot to learn and Thomas has said we can spend time there seeing how it runs as a hotel before it closes after the summer season.

He can give us all sorts of help in all the practicalities of running a business. And…' she looked at Des.

'We were wondering if you would like to join us in it? We'd need someone to do publicity, a website, take bookings, general admin, reception, that type of thing.'

'Right. I wasn't expecting that one…' Matt's mind travelled in the direction of Sophie. 'Kind of you to ask and it sounds great. Is it okay if I think about it for a bit?' (What on earth is happening here, he wondered.)

'Of course, Matt,' said Janice, stabilising her son's wobbly train of thought. 'It'll be a few months at least. There's a lot to think about before we'd actually open up and it would be good if maybe in a couple of months or so, when we've done some initial planning, we can talk about it a bit more?'

'Absolutely. That's fine,' said her somewhat distracted son.

'It's none of our business,' added Janice, 'but it's fine if you want to talk about this with Sophie and with her looking at a job too this may all have…'

'Implications.' said Matt completing her sentence.

Driving back from the visit, Sophie felt more confused than ever. She really liked the place and the job they were offering. Really liked it.

■ ■ ■

Matt had spent the whole of that evening waiting. Ever since Jo died he'd get anxious if someone was late. His mind motored at high speed past Delay Drive and Accident Avenue straight on to a dead end. Sophie had hoped to be home by nine. It was now 10.27.

Hi Matt, only just got back. Terrible traffic. S xx

Great. So glad to hear from you. ☺ I was really worried. How did it go? xx

Sorry. Thought you might be ☺ Couldn't find anywhere to stop. It was good to go but not sure I'm any clearer. How was it with your M&D? X

'Is it me she's not any clearer about?' he wondered.

Glad you're safe. It was good, thanks. Really exciting what they're planning. A lot to think about. Are you still off to Rosie's 2moro? x

'Would it affect us?' she thought.

Good. Yes, if that's OK. It'll be good to be there for Dad's anniversary. Back Sunday so see you then? X

Sunday will be great. Tilly at M&D so we'll have uninterrupted time. ☺ Lunch? X

Brill. Let's go out. Wish I could see you before. Sleep well ♥ Love you lots xxx

Me too. Love you xxx

Matt looked at the photo by his computer. Sophie looked back. He thought about how it was helpful that they were accepted as a couple at the local parish church – they'd decided to go there instead of his dad's to avoid tongues wagging. All the same, there was still the occasional comment towards Sophie about how difficult it must be looking after him. Matt was sure some thought Sophie was his carer – and one rather confused soul, the elderly Mrs Conway, thought her to be his daughter. There'd been the odd, 'Is it serious?' and 'When are you two getting married?' questions, which they brushed off, although the constant prying was becoming more irritating. There were others, though, often couples, who offered them Sunday lunch and said they were available to chat if they wanted: after all, they'd been there and done that. They were fellow travellers on a road.

He recalled how his parents had talked of their own marriage and wondered what his mum meant when she said about taking their time. He was glad it had been friendship first with Sophie. Albeit in different ways, they both needed time to come to terms with the past and all the baggage they still carried. He knew that in many ways he had the easier decision. If Sophie got the job, Tilly was young enough to up sticks and move before she started primary school. If they stayed put, being involved in his parents' project could be exciting and fulfilling. Whatever, the outcome, he still wanted to be with Sophie and that was clear.

CHAPTER 8

A reasonable risk

Memories of a much-loved, much-missed dad accompanied a winter woodland walk. It had been a difficult year and not just for Sophie and her sister. Rosie and Paul's children had found it hard losing their grandad especially as they couldn't remember a time when he hadn't been unwell.

Reaching a bench overlooking the hills, as they sat down Sophie said, 'You know what I'm like. I fancied Matt the first time I met him but professional boundaries and all that... And I was with the tennis coach then.' She laughed at her own seemingly unimportant afterthought. Sophie always referred to her exes by occupation: it helped dampen the memories.

'Then he left and I started getting involved with the policeman. What a mess. I couldn't believe it when Matt asked if he could see me as a friend. And I thought, you know what, Sophie Howlett, I don't want a lover, I just need a friend.'

'Texas!' shouted Paul.

'What?'

'Sorry, Soph. We have this silly thing that if someone says words from a song, we see who can be first to name the band,' her sister explained.

'Ah, what it is to have simple minds,' Sophie teased, resisting the urge to add 'Did you see what I did there?'.

'Anyway, as I was saying, and I know I've said this before, it is different with Matt. This time I feel more loved because of the way he's always there for me. I feel more secure because he's sound and reliable. And I feel more appreciated than with anyone else I've ever known – it's the little things he does for me and how he tells me how he feels about me.' Sophie paused in case her sister was laughing at her or shaking her head in that mocking way she sometimes did. She wasn't.

'The fly in the ointment is this whole job thing, Rosie. If I got it, I don't know if he'd come. If he did, I don't know if that would be fair on him and Tilly either, making them uproot and affecting her schooling and all that.'

'There may be a better job somewhere else, Soph, something may come up closer to home,' interjected her sister pragmatically. 'Do you want to be with him for life?'

'Straight in as usual, Rosemary,' laughed Sophie. 'I could see that happening. I do really like just being with him. I know what you're going to say: him being disabled and all that. And yes, it is frustrating not being able to do what other couples do or go to some places because of his wheelchair. And there's Tilly. She's a real sweetheart but having her around cramps our style a bit at times.'

'Tell us about it,' added Paul. 'We haven't finished a conversation for eight years.'

'It's good you can acknowledge the tougher bits, Soph,' her sister continued. 'As someone to take care of him, you're the best person he could ever hope for. But it's not going to get easier as you both get older. Marriage is far more than being a carer.'

'Yeah, I know. It's not easy now sometimes – there's been a couple of times when I've let my frustration show. Like when I was tired and stressed by the whole disciplinary thing. He was lovely about it but I felt bad. He gets frustrated too. We've cried together at what he can't do – and we've laughed at the funny things. Like when he's using his dumbbells and falls out the wheelchair. But I love him.'

'Does he compare you to Jo?' Rosie asked.

'I'd be surprised if he didn't,' Sophie replied. 'I certainly compare myself to her and I never even met her. But you know what, he's never said anything like "Jo did it this way" or "Jo would think that". He's never compared the two of us, at least he's not said as much.'

The cold was setting in. 'Have you talked about getting married?' Paul asked, as they walked on.

Sophie told them about what Tilly had said a couple of weeks ago: 'At least, neither of us leapt in said, "No, definitely not!" We touched on the subject afterwards but it felt a bit awkward and didn't talk about it any further, really. I think neither of us were sure what to say next – and we were too distracted by the job stuff, to be honest. I'd like to talk about it more, though. I really would.'.

'That's what we did,' said Paul. 'Quite gently to begin with. We went to see one or two married couples we knew and that was really helpful. It meant we were talking about marrying each other without the "awkwardness", if that's the right word, of talking to each other, if you get my drift.'

'Did you feel absolutely certain it was what you wanted?' asked Sophie.

'No', Rosie and Paul said in unison, laughing at the solidarity of their response. Rosie added: 'If someone was that sure, I'd be asking why they've not asked themselves some difficult questions.'

'Like the ones you've asked me?' responded Sophie, with a smile...

Rosie nodded. 'Name the elephants in the room and think about how you're going to tame them. Being married isn't always easy.'

Paul nodded. 'Absolutely.'

'Gee. Thanks, Paul.' Rosie smiled.

'One couple used the phrase "reasonable risk",' added Paul. 'If the wanting to be together outweighs the doubts about it… If you both feel you'd like to get married – for better for worse, in sickness and in health etcetera then…'

'What do you think I should do, Rosie?' Sophie asked.

'Well, I wouldn't ask my sister for a start,' she laughed.

The muddy path was wet. The winter sun found its way between the bare branches. Dappled light was bringing clarity.

■ ■ ■

The next day, Sophie and Matt sat in their favourite restaurant in the middle of town. A table for two overlooking the river welcomed the Sunday roast dinner they had been looking forward to.

'You first,' said Matt.

'Coward,' teased Sophie.

'Chivalrous,' joked Matt.

They talked.

They talked for the next couple of hours.

They talked for the next couple of weeks.

■ ■ ■

Sophie's colleagues were desperate to know who'd sent her red roses that Valentine's Day – and why there were only eight instead of a dozen. 'He was once in the Oxford and

Cambridge Boat Race,' she explained on more than one occasion, spelling out about the number of people in a rowing crew. Some got it; others didn't.

That evening, with Tilly tucked up in bed, they sat next to each other. Sophie, cushion across her chest, legs curled up and leaning against Matt. Each with a pen. Each holding a small piece of paper. Each writing their decision.

'You first,' said Matt. Sophie smiled. She'd heard that somewhere before. Folding it carefully, she handed over her piece of paper. Holding it in front of his face, he unfurled it slowly.

I've decided not to apply.

Matt raised his eyebrows in mock horror. He handed over his piece... and took it back. Sophie hit him with a cushion. He unfolded it. Folded it. Handed over again.

Will you marry me?

Sophie grabbed her piece back and turned it over.

Pen poised. Looking back and forth between paper and paramour.

Yes! Yes! Yes! Yes! Yes! Yes! Yes! Yes!

'Umm, eight times, eh?'

■　■　■

They kept things quiet for a fortnight (again). Sophie knew people who hated the engagement period: the constant questions and the pressure to have the 'perfect day'. Matt knew that all too well for himself and remembered how often he and Jo wished they had eloped. Sophie didn't want a 'big do' (unlike her sister, who both did and had). They'd both be happy with just family (including Jo's) and a few friends. Matt's parents were delighted to hear the news as were Jo's, and Rosie and Paul too (even if it wasn't a big do). Tilly would be told next but there was something else to do first.

Matt and Sophie were wrapped up against the cold March wind as it was funnelled by the High Street's red brick buildings. 'Click and Collect' at the out of town retail park had picked up the shops and taken them away. A third of the units were empty and charity shops filled some of the rest.

Standing between a newsagent and a, now closed, fashion boutique, J. Frampton, Jewellers was one of the few shops which had occupied a place for more than a decade. J. Frampton himself died at the turn of the century and his son had kept the shop ticking over by repairing clocks and watches. Behind its wooden-framed windows edged in peeling black paint, trays of rings sat in old grey, foam inserts. Each ring numbered. Each one priced.

Sophie's long blonde hair was blown about like a recalcitrant snood. 'What do you think about that one?' Matt suggested as they looked through the window at Tray 5 Number 303.

'No, don't think so,' Sophie replied. The same exchange was repeated six times. Only the numbers changed.

With a ring of the bell above the door, Michael Frampton emerged in a pinstripe with waistcoat, his jeweller's loupe precariously perched in his right eye. A pair of half-rimmed glasses hung on a chain around his neck. His grey-haired comb over quickly dismantled by the strengthening wind. He lived above the shop having bought the leasehold when his father died. As the sole employee, he took a modest salary and closed for lunch and half-day Wednesdays. He was in his mid-sixties and the shop would probably die when he did. 'Can I help you? I've got more inside if you'd like to come in,' he said to the window shoppers.

Sophie and Matt smiled awkwardly in the knowledge they'd been found out. They didn't fancy the look of the shop but accepted the offer as they didn't have the heart to refuse. After a bit of an effort, they managed to negotiate Matt's wheelchair through the door. The thin metal threshold causing particular difficulty. The inside of the shop was as old-fashioned as the window had presented it to be.

'How about these?' Michael Frampton asked as he pulled out a couple of trays from inside the glass fronted cabinet near the till. His two new customers looked in silence, pointing at a couple of rings in order to contradict their lack of enthusiasm. 'What is it you're looking for?' asked the shopkeeper, who had always prized good customer service.

Sophie blushed. 'We've just got engaged,' she said.

'Oh! My congratulations to both of you,' gushed Michael. 'It's such a joy to see a young couple take that step nowadays. There's been a real drop in people getting married, you know. So, diamond, sapphire, emerald or something a little less expensive?'

Sophie hadn't really thought about it, if she was honest. 'Umm… I just want one that looks nice on my finger,' she replied, realising that wasn't particularly helpful.

'Of course,' replied Michael, who'd heard it all before. 'May I have a look?'

Sophie stretched out her hand. 'I know just the thing,' he said decidedly. 'Just a moment…. Now, Tray 12, Number 207,' he muttered to himself. Michael was very proud of the numbering system he'd brought in when he took over the shop nearly twenty years ago. It hadn't changed since. He placed Tray 12 in front of the happy couple. 'How about this one?' he said proudly, pointing to a high-quality diamond with a matching price.

'It's a bit…' Matt began to reply.

'Only joking,' laughed Michael. 'No,' he winked. 'This one.' Number 207 was a small blue sapphire set in a silver ring with a more realistic price tag. 'Would you like to try it on?' Michael asked Sophie. Sliding it on to her long, narrow third finger, a little nudge took it over the knuckle.

Sophie was taken aback by unexpected tears. 'It's beautiful. Thank you.'

Matt wiped some dust that had suddenly appeared in his left eye. 'Yes, it's lovely. Looks great on you. Would you like it?'

Sophie nodded. 'Well, I don't think it needs any adjustment, but we'll just check, shall we,' said Michael. After ensuring customer satisfaction was satisfied, Michael offered them terms or they could pay straight away.

'We'll pay now if that's okay,' said Matt in the knowledge that Rob and Gill McKenzie's kindness meant they could afford it.

Returning to the flat, they could see Tilly sat next to her grandma. 'Sophie!' shouted Tilly in her usual way, running up and giving her a hug before climbing on to her dad's lap.

'Well, Tilly,' said Matt. 'We've got something to tell you.'

Tilly's eyes opened wide as she glimpsed a flash of blue on Sophie's hand. 'Are you going to be my new Mummy?'

Sophie laughed, as did the others. 'Yes, Tilly. I am.'

She jumped on to the floor. 'Yay! Are you going to have a wedding with a big dress and lots of flowers? Are you going to have a big car too? Can I be your bridesmaid? I'd like a blue dress please and flowers in my hair. Can I? Can I?' shouted Tilly as she jumped around, her newly braided hair bouncing in unison with her excitement.

Matt smiled and nodded. 'Yes, all those things, Tilly. Just for you,' said Sophie.

■ ■ ■

Will Taylor was next to know. Ever since Matt was in hospital, the two of them spoke every Thursday evening. Occasionally, Will made the ninety-minute journey to Eastwood Minster and they'd go to the pub by the river. The former Best Man was the only one to know how Matt felt about the blossoming friendship with Sophie and his hopes that it may develop into something more. A confirmed bachelor, Will listened to the joys and the dilemmas about the future with both patience and detachment. Even though he'd dropped the rings down a heating grate at Matt and Jo's wedding, Will was the obvious choice. 'Twice? It'll be a joy and an honour, my man,' he'd said in his posh, plummy accent when Matt asked him.

Told to do 'Greats' by his parents, the Duke and Duchess of Tainton, The Honourable William Taylor was out of his depth at Oxford: unlike the boats he rowed in. Poor results in assignments and exams led to lecturers calling him the University's contribution to energy conservation. Will often described himself as being like one of his father's classic racing cars: great looks but hopeless on the open road. The rowing provided a lifeline to hide a struggle with depression, which nobody had taken seriously until a suicide attempt.

It was the day when the crew selections for the Boat Race were announced. Matt was in the Blue Boat but Will was out – not even in Isis. He was devastated. All those early mornings and late evenings. All that time in muscle-wrenching gym sessions. The Fours. The Trial VIIIs. He was told it was tactical. He'd become the failure his father always said he would be.

The Boat House stored lots of rope and Will had slung one over a roof joist. Securing one end to a pillar and tying a noose in the other, he stood on a carefully positioned chair. Distracted by the sound of a key in the lock, Will looked towards the door with desperation in his eyes. Matt ran in and flung his arms around Will's waist and lifted him down. They sat there on the floor. Will sobbing, Matt with his arms around him, rocking gently.

Will got help after that. It was too late to save his degree course although Matt's actions certainly saved his life - and that was all because Matt had left his gloves in the Boat House. Had he not gone back to get them, well, neither of them wanted to think about what would have happened. It was a day neither of them would forget.

Matt supported Will through the months of recovery that followed and Will had returned the privilege in the last three years. Will knew recovery from mental health problems didn't mean the complete absence of symptoms and he still experienced occasional times of anxiety and depression. Life wasn't always easy for him and his father didn't help matters by constantly reminding him what he could have achieved. Glad to have an elder brother and not to be the 'son and heir', Will was happy with the person he was now and that was all that mattered.

■   ■   ■

The local vicar, Reverend Liz James was delighted to be asked to marry them. With Sophie's deadlines for her Masters and a completed second draft of Matt's new book due in June, they opted for the first Saturday in July. Des West would give the address and the gospel choir would sing. Thomas Southcott offered them free use of a function room and the four-poster suite for their first night. With only thirty guests, it would be just the kind of day Sophie and Matt wanted.

'It's your day. No one else's,' the vicar told them. 'Don't let others make it into something you don't want. I'm afraid I've seen so many couples – and their friends and families – place so much emphasis on the day itself, they forget what it is they're actually doing.'

The news was out by the following Sunday evening's service. They were swamped by well-wishers. Some simply grabbed Sophie's hand to look at the ring. Nothing else. Just the ring. The attention was enjoyable but they were glad when the service started.

Matt had never heard Sophie swear very often. 'You okay?' he asked somewhat unnecessarily.

'No,' she replied, feeling anxiety trying to get its claws in to her. 'Look. Over there. Sat at the end of the pew. Other side. Two rows in front of ours.'

Matt nodded. 'Tall man. Short hair?'

'That's him. It's the policeman. What on earth is he doing here?'

'Ah. Okay. Do you want to go home?'

'No,' Sophie replied, distracted by Dave Rawlinson encroaching into her safe space. 'Thanks. Just a bit of shock. Maybe leave during the last hymn?'

Mrs Conway was sat in front of them. She turned around and looked. 'Young people these days. Don't know how to behave in church,' she said loudly to the person next to her, as the organ played the first hymn. 'Always talking after the service has started.'

When it was over, more people stopped to offer their congratulations as Matt and Sophie tried to leave. Mrs Conway came over for a second look: 'Who's the lucky man, dear?' she asked Matt.

'Hello Sophie.' The voice from behind sent a shiver down her spine. Her mind thrown back to what happened all those months ago. She hadn't eaten pizza since and it wasn't because she didn't like it. She didn't want to turn around but knew she must.

'Remember me?' he said.

'How could I forget?' Sophie replied. Matt turned and smiled at him. 'Fancy seeing you here,' Sophie continued after an awkward few seconds. 'Is this personal or business?' She tried not to be cold but it was hard to be warm.

Dave Rawlinson laughed. 'Business actually – not police though. I've left. And you?' he said, looking at Matt expecting her to reply in the same vein.

'This is Matt. My fiancé.' Sophie had served an Ace.

'Oh, I see. Well, congratulations,' he replied, missing the return by a long way.

'Thank you. Well, we must be off now, I'm afraid,' although not nearly as afraid as the last time she saw him.

'Sophie,' interjected Dave before she could escape his clutches once again. 'I wish to apologise for what I did last year. To be honest it should have brought me to my senses too. It's a long story, but soon afterwards, I was dismissed from the Force – and yes, before you ask it was to do with a female colleague. Not my proudest moments.'

Sophie nodded. 'Sorry to hear that,' she said as genuinely as she could. 'Thank you for the apology, though, I appreciate that.' Match point.

'Don't worry,' Dave Rawlinson replied. 'You won't see me here again. I've just got to see someone over there who I arranged to meet here. They're moving in to my house tomorrow and then it's goodbye Eastwood Minster. London calling. Good luck.' He smiled awkwardly and looked at Matt. 'You're more deserving of her than me.'

Leaving the church, the cold March wind brought relief to the heat of the last few minutes.

'Drink?' Matt asked Sophie as they moved down the ramp.

'Domino's?'

CHAPTER 9

The power of love

The usual pre-wedding practicalities took shape: sometimes square, other times circular and just occasionally, dodecahedron. Invitations sent, service sheets printed and music choices composed.

Sophie had to tone down Rosie's designs on a wedding dress and they compromised on the shade of blue for the two bridesmaids. It was an unexpected surprise that Rosie's son was happy with his page boy suit. Mrs Conway and her team of flower arrangers brought ideas which pruned the couple's prejudices about her. The lady who so often presented as confused came to life as she told them about the four times she and her late husband won Gold Medals in the Floral Marquee at Chelsea forty years previously.

Planning how Sophie's belongings would fit into Matt's flat was particularly time consuming. Living in a one-bedroom furnished apartment over a hairdresser in the High Street was hardly a cut above but she'd made it her home and had acquired a lot of possessions during the previous five years. She and Matt couldn't afford to buy anywhere and they knew they'd be hard pushed to find a larger, wheelchair-friendly place but hoped the Housing Association may help in time.

Matt's publisher returned the second draft with some edits and wanted more work done on the introduction. Sophie's Master's assignments were taxing as were increasing demands at work. Together with Tilly getting ready to move on from pre-school, it all made for a rather stressful period – let alone preparing to be married. They looked forward to being on the other side of a Saturday in July.

As pleasant and customer focussed as ever, Michael Frampton guided them to a range of gold wedding rings. 'Matching ones are very popular,' he told them.

After they had decided on the signs of their marriage, he said: 'May I ask you something more personal, Mr West? I believe you are the son of the minister at the Pentecostal Church? Well, through the Chamber of Commerce, I know Thomas Southcott and I understand he is considering giving his hotel to the church for a bereavement support centre? That is such a wonderful idea. It is so needed. I lost my wife three years ago.'

Sophie put her hand on Matt's shoulder.

'It was so devastating. We had no children and while my business colleagues and customers were lovely, I so wish I had had other support at that time. I still do now, to be honest,' he laughed self-consciously. 'I wish your parents great success with it. Who knows I may even come along.'

'Please do, Mr Frampton,' replied Matt.

'Michael. Please. Michael.'

'Please do… Michael. You will be very welcome. We all need support at such times and in the years that follow, don't we? Hopefully, it'll be open in the Autumn,' he said, putting his hand on to Sophie's.

■　■　■

Ever since they became engaged, Matt knew there was one thing he had to do before their wedding day.

The memory of the steep hillside graveyard was crystal clear. There was no way he would get there in his wheelchair. That was one of the reasons which had stopped him from going before now. There were others. He'd always found it difficult that he wasn't at the funeral. There had been many times when he regretted agreeing to Jo being buried so far away but no one was thinking particularly clearly at the time. He remembered feeling it would be better for Rob and Gill that Jo was nearer to them, although he hadn't considered the impact on himself or Tilly for when she was older. He'd been to his grandparents' funerals and often thought what it must have been like for Jo's family walking in after the coffin. The pain of those left behind in plain sight of everyone else.

Sat in the passenger seat of Rob McKenzie's Jaguar, the conversation quietened as they approached the Cotswold village church. The anniversary was as poignant as the previous two. It had been a long journey – and not just the two and a half hours it had taken them that morning. Matt hadn't been for six years. Rob hadn't been for six days.

'Does it get any easier?' Matt asked.

'No, not at the moment,' Rob replied sadly. 'I guess it will. Some day. The scare about Penny set us both back and it's tough seeing others move on with their lives and we're not. Don't get me wrong, Matt, we're absolutely delighted about you and Sophie. We really are. Gill said something the other day which was helpful, though. She heard someone on the radio talking about the loss of their child. "The hole never gets smaller," this woman said. "But beautiful things grow around the edge of it." Helpful that. I think I'll try and look for them a bit more.'

'We had to fight for it,' Rob continued as they pulled into the car park. 'In the end they let us have a plot on the lower bit of land which is much flatter. We wanted to lay her there as we knew you'd get here one day.'

Matt absorbed this sudden alteration to his assumptions and wished he'd known that before.

Going through the lychgate, they followed the cream, Cotswold stone gravel path, Rob pushing when the wheels got in too deep. Moving on to the undulating grass was tricky but they managed.

Matt laid the flowers on the grave.

'Take as long you like,' Rob said as he left Matt by himself. 'I do.'

Josephine Mary West
Aged 27
Beloved wife of Matthew
& mother of Matilda.
Daughter of Robert & Gillian.
Always loved, never forgotten.

It was strange seeing the names in full. Even Matt had forgotten she was Josephine. Everyone assumed she was Joanne. 'Hello Jo,' he said. 'Sorry I've not made it before.' A granite headstone looked back. He knew she wasn't there but it was good to talk to her. Just like he had with the photo.

When he was here six years ago, Jo arrived in a big black car and emerged in a gorgeous white dress, with a bouquet of flowers. Three years later, she came in another black car, coming out in a box, with a bouquet of flowers.

Birds singing and the warmth of the June sunshine on his back helped ease the pain as he talked. His books and his parents' plans. Tilly and Sophie (checking Jo was alright with it – again). About the hopes they had had and the ones he now held. His lasting sadness for the loss of the woman who lay there.

After half an hour, he waved to Rob and watched his father-in-law walk towards him carrying scissors and a watering can. Matt looked one more time at the grave: 'Goodbye Jo.'

He was ready to move on.

■　■　■

A week or so later, Michael Frampton stood across the road from St Mark's Church sheltering in the pouring rain under a large blue and white golfing umbrella. It was his lunch break as he watched the specially hired 1931 six-seater Renault Landaulette draw up outside.

Sophie, Rosie and the twins enjoyed travelling in it from Thomas Southcott's hotel where they had all spent the night. Tilly's face was a picture of astonishment and excitement when the car picked her up from her grandparents. 'It's just like Chitty, Chitty, Bang, Bang!' she exclaimed.

Wearing a chauffer's uniform, but without a servant's attention to detail, Paul had forgotten the umbrellas. For a few minutes he was not as popular as he would have liked to have been. The vicar and verger came bearing brollies and the largest choir robes they could muster to shelter everyone from the torrent. Sophie had promised Matt she wouldn't be late and she wasn't: it's just that it took ten minutes to dry off and readjust their dresses.

'Look at my flowers!' shouted Tilly, as a window reflected the damage done to her headdress. Her blue dress crumpled and damp, she sat on the floor in the entrance lobby refusing to move. 'I'm not doing it. I want my real Mummy,' she screamed.

'But Sophie is…,' began Rosie, before being touched by her sister's restraining hand.

The kerfuffle could be heard inside the church. Matt turned towards the noise. His mum asked, 'Shall I go?'

Matt, cool as anything, announced to the whole congregation: 'There seems to be a slight local difficulty. Excuse me one moment.' Everyone laughed as he wheeled himself down the aisle, spotting two familiar faces sat right at the very back as he did so.

Seeing him approaching, Sophie was quickly ushered out of sight. Funny how the vicar believed in bad luck, she thought. Seconds later, Tilly was sat on her dad's lap, burying her head in his chest. Buttonhole crushed. A wet patch on his Moss Bros suit.

'You can have mine, Tilly,' said Rosie's daughter, without prompting. Tilly's face lit up as the new arrangement was carefully placed. Tissues dried her dampened cheeks and a tickle under the chin rendered the downturned lips redundant.

'Right then, Til,' said Matt. She loved it when he called her that. 'Shall we go in?' Sat on his lap, they went up the aisle together. Faces beaming, they received a round of applause. 'You sit with Grandma, eh?'

'Please would you stand,' announced The Reverend Liz James.

'How are you going to do that one, Matt?' whispered Will Taylor in a beautifully judged quip.

With Rosie on her left, Sophie's off-the-shoulder, floor length, ivory dress turned every head as her steps moved up the aisle in time to Pachelbel's Canon. Turning around, Matt was lost for words as he watched her approaching.

About two-thirds of the way up, Rosie stopped. Sophie looked with a puzzled expression, as her sister put her left hand on the shoulder of an elderly gentleman stood, stooping at the end of a row. He turned his face towards them: 'May I have the honour, young Sophie, lass?'

'Grandad!' Sophie exclaimed, her voice rising high above the sound of the music. Walking stick in his left hand, he crooked his right arm to welcome the bride. Sophie saw her grandma smiling broadly from the next chair along. Rosie passed Sophie a hankie. It was her turn to be lost for words. They walked on in perfect time as the music repeated its joyful pattern.

On reaching the front, Sophie leant down to Matt and kissed him on the cheek: 'Did you know about this?' He smiled and shook his head. 'Do you want one?' she said, passing him the hankie. They laughed.

'Now, lad, you look after this young lady,' Sophie's Grandad said in his broad Yorkshire accent. 'She's a real treasure, this one.' He turned to face the Vicar: 'Now, Reverend, I'm giving her away but I need to go and sit down. My legs aren't as good as they used to be. You know all about that, don't you, lad,' he added to Matt with a cheeky smile. The congregation applauded as Rosie walked him back to his wife of sixty-six years.

'We have come together.'

■　■　■

It was the morning after the night before. Sophie and Matt lay together in the plush and comfortable four-poster. They'd talked all evening about everything that happened. How, after eating fish and chips for tea by the river, Matt and Tilly spent the rest of Friday playing 'weddings'. Sophie was Barbie and Matt was an Action Man with bendy legs so he could sit down. The Vicar was played by Clara the Camel and Tilly was herself. Sophie admitted she'd been sad that her dad wasn't there to walk her up the aisle but the surprise of her grandparents was overwhelming. It was Rosie and Paul who organised all that: the vicar was the only one in on it.

Tilly's tantrum had relaxed everyone's nerves. Supported by Will and a crutch, Matt stood for the vows and exchanging of rings. His father gave the best wedding address anyone had heard since Harry and Meghan. 'This is the power of love,' Des said as he held back his tears from all they'd been through in the last three years.

The gospel choir sang Billy Joel's 'Just the way you are' and Aretha Franklin's 'A Natural Woman' during the signing of the Registers (or the Singing of the Registers as the service sheet put it). There was the surprise of seeing Ian and Greg at the back. Both suited. Both smiling. Both clean shaven. Jane Wilson was there too, as were a couple of other colleagues from the hospital. Even Mrs Conway came. She congratulated Will Taylor as she left: 'I hope you'll be very happy,' she said.

Will didn't drop the rings but did have an anxiety attack before his speech. Mental ill health always leaves its mark. After fresh air and reassurance, he delivered it faultlessly. Having eaten their ice creams (two scoops), the reception party were in stitches over his reminiscences of some uni incidents that even Matt had forgotten about. He had them in tears with a glowing tribute to his best friend and sensitive reflection of all that had happened. Matt strung together several song titles to express his love for his bride, which had everyone reaching for the tissues again. The guests applauded Sophie as she used her speech to talk lovingly about her husband and everyone who had supported them. She was the one to mention Jo and how she wished she had known her: 'I'll look after him, Jo,' she said. Rob and Gill McKenzie brought Sophie and Matt to tears and laughter by their genuine delight at what was taking place. Tilly threw her headdress in to the air and Rosie's son caught it.

And now they were wrapped in each other's arms. Sophie's head lay resting on Matt's chest. It's gentle rise and fall accompanied by a rhythmic heartbeat. Hands stroking hands. Comfort. Security. Warmth.

'You know what, Mrs West?'

Sophie laughed at hearing her new name. 'What, Mr West?'

'It's not going to work.'

He paused.

'No. Definitely not. I just can't do it that way. I'll have to think of something else.'

Sophie raised her head to look at him. 'Oh, I don't know…'

'No. It has to be different,' he sighed.

He lay there, trying to be serious. The tightening of his chest betraying the laughter he was holding in.

'Matt West. What are you talking about?'

'The novel. It's just not the right opening.'

He felt a pillow hit him in the face.

Acknowledgements

Firstly, I want to thank you, the reader. I hope you enjoyed it. It's people like you who provide such valuable support for independent publishers and booksellers.

Secondly, while, yes, this is a work of fiction and any resemblance etcetera is indeed coincidental, I also want to thank the many people who, in the course of my work and personal life, enabled me to play a small part in their story and have inspired much of this one. They have taught me so much about what it means to move on.

I'd like also to thank Pam and George Norman, Helen Box and Sue Banham for kindly reading an early draft and providing such valuable comments which helped shape the story. Thank you also to Taryn Johnston at Chronos Publishing for her encouragement, advice and wise observations which brought these words to your hands.

Finally, where would I be without Jane and our two wonderful offspring, Jon and Rachel. Their affirmation and encouragement has been and always is invaluable.

About the Author

Richard Frost spent most of his paid employment career helping people to find or remain in work. He specialised in helping those whose had a disability or other health conditions and, in particular, people who experienced depression, anxiety and mental ill health. He was appointed a MBE for Services To Mental Health in 2018.

Married to Jane, who is a vicar, Richard is a lay minister in the Church of England and the author of Finding Stability in Times of Change (Endulini Publishing 2022) and Life with St Benedict (BRF 2019). He writes a blog at workrestpray.com.

They live in Devon and Looking to Move On is Richard's debut novel.

richardfrostauthor.com

Credits

Lyrics from the following songs have been included or alluded to within this story and copyright, where known, remains with those shown:

'*A New England*' by Billy Bragg 1983

'*American Pie*' by Don McLean 1971

'*Brimful Of Asha*' by Tejinder Singh Nurpuri (Cornershop) 1997

'*Comfortably Numb*' by David Gilmour, Roger Waters (Pink Floyd) 1979

'*Dignity*' by Ricky Ross (Deacon Blue) 1987

'*Fix You*' by Guy Berryman, Jonny Buckland, Will Champion, Chris Martin (Coldplay) 2005

'*I Don't Want A Lover*' by Sharleen Spiteri, John Mcelphone (Texas) 1989

'*Single Ladies*' by Terius Nash, Beyoncé Knowles, Thaddis Harrell, Chris Stewart 2008

'*Three Little Birds*' by Bob Marley 1977